THE SIREN'S REALM

THE TETHERING, BOOK TWO

MEGAN O'RUSSELL

Ink Worlds Press

Visit our website at www.MeganORussell.com

The Siren's Realm

Cover Art by Sleepy Fox Studio (https://www.sleepyfoxstudio.net/)

Editing by Christopher Russell

Interior Design by Christopher Russell

Printed in the United States of America

DEDICATION

To all the friends who wander with me,
whether or not we're lost

THE SIREN'S REALM

1

BOUND

*T*he cool autumn air crept through the house. The trees in the garden had not yet begun to change their leaves, but they seemed to know their time was coming.

Inside the house was silence. As the afternoon sun peered through the window, all it saw was stillness. Emilia sat at her desk in the big library, staring at a page in a little brown book.

TETHERING

The magical binding of two people. Historically, tethering was an integral part of a wizarding wedding. After a tethering ceremony, the coniunx, *or tethered couple, would gain the ability to sense one another and would develop a greatly increased emotional attachment.*

In today's wizarding society, tethering is rarely included in wedding ceremonies. It is generally considered archaic and makes divorce much more difficult, as a tethering can only be severed by the death of one of the coniunx. *The demise of half of the pair is incredibly painful for the remaining party and often results in their subsequent death.*

Throughout wizarding history, some have used tethering as a weapon. By forcing a slave, captive, or unwilling bride to be tethered to a new master, the spellcaster would ensure the forcibly tethered party would be unlikely to attempt escape, and should an escape occur, tracking the coniunx *would be simple. Forced tethering was made illegal in 1813 as a part of the International Wizarding Agreement and is punishable by the severest penalty allowable in the nation in which the offense occurs.*

Captive. Unable to escape. How many times had she read that page in the few months since Graylock? Five hundred, maybe six? Reading the passage never made it any better. Still, she began the page again, hoping the words would somehow be different.

Tethering—The magical binding of two—

The front door crashed open, and an excited shout of "Emilia!" carried down the hall followed closely by, "Claire, don't break the door!"

Emilia slipped the book into the desk drawer before Claire tore around the corner and into the library.

"Emilia!" she squealed, her bright blond hair falling from her ponytail, and her cheeks red from excitement and the wind. "You missed the best thing ever! I helped Jacob with his shield spells, and I sparred with Connor and won!"

Claire began an energetic victory dance as Jacob and Connor entered the library. Connor limped in with a grimace on his face, and Jacob failed to suppress a smile.

"Yes, Claire," Connor said through clenched teeth as he lowered himself into his desk chair, "you did a great job."

"What's that you say?" Claire leaned in toward Connor, her hand cupped around her ear. "You just got beat by a twelve-year-old?"

Emilia smiled, knowing it was what Claire wanted to see. Aunt Iz had always believed that all witches and wizards should know how to defend themselves. Sparring had been a part of the education received at the Mansion House for as long as Emilia could remember, but daily practice hadn't begun until after Graylock. That's how life felt now, split into two pieces—before Graylock, and after.

Emilia noticed Claire's mouth moving. She bounced around,

giving a blow by blow of how she had beaten Connor. Claire stood on the back of the couch before launching herself onto Connor.

Emilia forced herself to laugh as cheerfully as she could manage. "That's great, Claire." She hoped her voice didn't sound too unnaturally high.

"Let's go get some dinner," Jacob said, lifting Claire off Connor, taking her by the shoulders and steering her toward the hall.

"But I want to talk to Emilia." Claire twisted away from Jacob's grasp.

"Later," Jacob said firmly. He jerked his head for Connor to follow and led Claire out of the library.

Emilia laid her forehead on her desk. The wood felt cool on her face. She should follow them. It was time for dinner. Molly would be waiting, but other faces would be missing. Everywhere she went in the house, someone was missing.

Emilia's heart started to race. She took a deep breath, but in her mind all she could see was flames. And Samuel and Dexter. They should be here. But Samuel was gone, and Dexter was a traitor.

"Emi." Jacob touched her back, sending her heart racing again, but in such a different way. She sat up and looked into Jacob's bright blue eyes.

"They're waiting for you," Jacob said, pulling his hand back as Emilia shrugged away from his touch.

"Sure." Emilia stood and started for the kitchen, but as she passed the dining room, a chorus of voices shouted, "Happy birthday!"

Aunt Iz, Molly, Professor Eames, Connor, and Claire all stood around the table looking at her. Emilia stared at them.

"You didn't think we would forget your birthday?" Aunt Iz asked, walking over to Emilia and pulling her into a warm hug.

"No, of course not." Emilia blinked away her confusion. She

didn't think they had forgotten her birthday, but she hadn't remembered it herself.

"Come sit!" Claire dragged Emilia away from Iz and pushed her into her seat at the table.

"Our little girl is seventeen already." Molly bustled out of the room, dabbing her face on her apron, and returned moments later with large plates of food hovering in front of her. As though held by invisible butlers, the plates all laid themselves down on the table with perfect synchronization. She hadn't cooked a meal like this since before Graylock.

"Claire worked all morning on the decorations," Connor said, pointing over Emilia's head and rolling his eyes as he began to eat.

Emilia twisted in her seat. A pink sign that had *Happy Birthday Emilia!!!!!!!!* written in glitter hung over the door. Pink confetti swirled through the air like snow, and three foot wide pink balloons bounced along the ceiling. The only concession to the fact that pink was not, in fact, Emilia's favorite color was the sole lavender balloon tied to the back of her chair.

Emilia looked around the room. Iz smiled back at her from the end of the table. Her grey hair was tied back in an elegant twist as always, but she looked older than she should. Her face was weathered with lines that had not been there a few months ago. Next to her sat Molly, covered with a light dusting of flour, her greying red hair falling out of its bun.

Next to Molly was Connor, her nephew, with bright red hair to match hers. Molly piled heaps of food onto his plate, continuously tutting about him growing too quickly, and she was right. He was fourteen and tall for his age. He had grown another two inches this month.

On Emilia's other side sat Claire, shaking her head at Professor Eames. The professor was shorter than everyone but Claire. His shrunken frame betrayed his age, but his toady little face was split in a wide grin as he chuckled and Claire giggled.

And Jacob. His dark blond hair needed cutting again. His bright blue eyes twinkled as he listened to Claire trying to explain something to the professor through her laughter.

Emilia knew they were all trying. They were being cheerful for her sake, giving her a happy birthday. But Emilia couldn't look away from the empty places at the table.

Claire had carried Dexter's chair to the yard and set fire to it months ago, as soon as she found out what Dexter had done. But Samuel's seat was still waiting for him at the table, like he was running late to her party and would come bounding in from the garden any minute.

Emilia talked with the family while they ate. Lessons they had done lately. Stories from when Molly was young. Perfectly normal conversation.

Molly brought out a huge cake covered with tiny flowers. In the center of each blossom was a candle burning with a vivid blue flame. As Emilia blew out the candles, each of the flowers floated into the air, joining the confetti that soared endlessly around the room, weaving in and out of the glistening chandelier.

"It's beautiful, Molly," Emilia said.

"Open your presents!" Claire shoved a box into Emilia's hands.

The box was small and covered in pale blue velvet. As Emilia opened it, her breath caught in her throat. Inside was a delicate silver ring with a tree of life, the crest of the Gray Clan, carved into the front.

"To replace the one that was lost," Iz said quietly. "I had it made by the same jeweler."

"Thank you, Aunt Iz." Emilia pushed her face into a smile.

"Now you can use it as your talisman again," Claire said, taking the ring out of the box and shoving it onto Emilia's finger.

"Maybe." Emilia touched the sapphire pendant around her neck. "I think I might try out my necklace a while longer."

Claire wrinkled her forehead.

"I love the ring, Aunt Iz. Thank you." Emilia stood and went over to Aunt Iz. She hugged her tight, trying to put so many things she hadn't been able to say into her arms.

"Jacob has a present for you, too," Claire said, handing Emilia a bigger box as soon as she broke away from Iz.

"Thank you, Jacob," Emilia said as she tore the white, sparkling paper off the box.

Inside was a mobile made of the brightest green leaves. As she pulled it out of the box, the leaves began to spin slowly as though blown by a gentle breeze. A sprig of lilac, Emilia's favorite flower, sat still at the very center as everything else rotated around.

Emilia remembered a night when Jacob had first come to the Mansion House, when he had first learned he was a wizard.

"Making the leaves fly was the first piece of magic you showed me here," Jacob said, pink creeping into his cheeks. "I put a *viriduro* spell on it so the flowers will always stay fresh."

"Well done." The professor leaned in to inspect the mobile.

"Thank you," Emilia said, touching Jacob's arm. His eyes met hers, and she pulled her hand away, sliding the mobile back into the box.

After an hour of dinner, Emilia's face ached from smiling. She hadn't spent that much time with anyone in months. Her brain felt heavy and tired from so much talking.

Molly had given her a new dress and a box of peanut brittle, and the professor had given her a new book on early African Wizards. When Molly finally started clearing the table, Emilia slipped away, running up the stairs to her room before anyone could call her back.

Emilia opened her bedroom window, letting the cold air fill the room. Thousands of stars peered back at her. The trees rustled in the breeze.

She lay down, gazing up at the canopy of her bed, trying to ignore the pull in her chest that told her to go and find Jacob. If she were with him, her heart said, everything would be all right. If she were with him, she would be safe.

Emilia gazed at the silver ring on her finger. She twisted her hand, watching the etched tree of life glint in the light. Where was her other ring, the one Iz had given her when she was seven? Had it been tossed aside in some cave? Was someone else using it as a talisman now? Using her ring to hurt people?

Jacob had given her a different ring to defend herself. One that felt almost exactly like this one. The same smooth band, the same feel on her hand.

Leaping off the bed, Emilia yanked open her dresser drawer and dug into the back corner where she had hidden the other silver ring. That ring had been contaminated, something found in an evil place. She had tossed it into the drawer without looking at it, wanting desperately to get it out of her sight.

Emilia's fingers closed on the cold metal, and she pulled the ring from the stacks of clothes. A silver ring, identical to hers except for the carving. Where hers had a tree, this ring had a tiny bird. A fist closed around her heart.

"Emilia!"

Footsteps thundered up the stairs. Cries of "Emilia!" and "Jacob, what's wrong?" echoed through the house.

Emilia's door burst open, and Jacob raced through, followed closely by Claire and Connor.

Jacob knelt next to Emilia, taking her face in his hands. She hadn't even noticed she was crying until he brushed the tears off her cheek.

"What's wrong?" he whispered.

"What's happening?" Aunt Iz asked as she and Molly panted into the room. The professor wheezed as he shuffled up next to them.

"I never looked at it." Emilia shook her head. Blond hair and a smiling rosy face swam through her mind. She held the ring out to Iz. "I put it away so I wouldn't have to see it. And now it's been so long." Emilia's voice cracked.

Iz took the ring and gasped.

"What?" Claire snatched the ring from Iz. Her eyes widened as they fell on the little bird. "Larkin. This is Larkin's ring. Why do you have Larkin's ring? She's missing. Did she leave it for you here? Is it a message from her?" Claire began tearing through Emilia's drawers. "She might have left something else. Larkin would leave us a clue so we could find her."

"She didn't leave it," Jacob said, wrapping an arm around Claire and pulling her away from the dresser. "I found that ring at Graylock."

"She was there," Emilia whispered. "That's why Samuel asked if we were alone. That's why he went back. To find her."

Larkin had been like a big sister to her, her protector. The Gray student who had become one of the elite MAGI Agents who protected order in the magical world.

Emilia yanked her hands through her hair. "He was going to save her, and we left both of them behind. Jacob, we left them."

"Emi." Jacob reached for her.

"We left them!" Emilia screamed, backing away from all of them. They didn't understand. It was her fault. Larkin was supposed to be indestructible. But MAGI had been ransacked by the Dragons, and Larkin taken at Graylock. Emilia had left them there. Samuel and Larkin, trapped in the dark. Her heart pounded in her chest, and sweat slicked her palms.

"Emilia, breathe," Aunt Iz said softly, just as she had when Emilia was little and lost control of her magic. But it wasn't Emilia who was spinning out of control. It was all of them. It was the world.

The mirror over Emilia's dresser shattered. Connor grabbed Claire and knocked her to the floor. Iz covered her head, the professor yelped, and Molly screamed. Jacob didn't flinch as he stared at Emilia.

"*Reparactus,*" Jacob murmured, and the pieces of glass flew through the air back into their frame. Within seconds, the cracks in the mirror disappeared as if it had never been broken.

Emilia looked into the mirror at an unfamiliar face. The long black hair was hers, but the grey eyes were wild and afraid.

"We will find a way to get Samuel and Larkin back," Aunt Iz said, walking to Emilia and wrapping her arms around her.

"They've been in there for months. If you couldn't find a way to get Samuel out, how are you going to get two people out? It's my fault," Emilia choked.

Molly and the professor herded Claire and Connor out of the room. Jacob slipped out behind them.

"None of this would have happened," Emilia struggled to speak but couldn't get the words out through her gasping tears.

The sheets folded back as Aunt Iz guided her to bed, tucking her in as she had done when Emilia was little. But warm blankets couldn't keep the monsters away. Not anymore.

2

CLAIRE'S GIFT

*E*milia couldn't sleep. She could feel Jacob upstairs, waiting to be sure she was all right. The voices that traveled through the hall were hushed, as though Emilia were a patient with a fatal illness.

Hours passed.

The stars traveled outside her window. Emilia forced herself to breathe, willing herself to remain calm. She didn't want Jacob to come running.

The floorboard outside Emilia's room squeaked.

There was a light tap on the door, and Claire called softly, "Emilia, can I come in?"

Emilia pulled her covers up over her head. She was warm, and it was quiet. Her desire to be left alone warred against how hurt Claire's feelings would be if she ignored her.

"Emilia, are you awake?" Claire's voice came again.

Emilia forced herself to sit up, turned on the light, and arranged her face into a smile. "Come on in."

Claire poked her blond head around the door. Her forehead was furrowed, and her mouth set in a scowl.

"What's up?" Emilia asked.

Claire sat down next to Emilia on the pale purple comforter, clutching her pink laptop to her chest.

"Are you okay?" Claire asked, examining Emilia's face.

"I'm fine." Emilia hoped it sounded true.

"I have a birthday present for you, but I need to make sure you won't freak out and break anything," Claire said in an unusually businesslike tone.

"I promise not to hurt your computer," Emilia said.

Claire nodded, apparently satisfied, and loosened her grip on the pink laptop. "Good, but nobody can know about this. If Iz found out, I'd be dead or sent away in a second."

Emilia's face fell. "Claire, what did you do?"

"I didn't really *do* anything. I'm just not actually supposed to have it." Claire's voice dripped with guilt.

"Did you steal something from Iz?" Emilia asked.

"Not from Iz."

"Claire!"

"Shhh!" Claire clapped a hand over Emilia's mouth. "And it wasn't stealing as much as salvaging. When you were…away, and MAGI was attacked, Aunt Iz asked me to crash the Spellnet database. With no one in the MAGI offices to make sure the system was secure, anyone could have hacked into the files, taken whatever information they wanted, and no one would have known."

"You crashed Spellnet?" Emilia asked, impressed despite herself at Claire's computer skills.

"Absolutely. Really, it was a piece of cake. MAGI wasn't as up on their security as they should have been, so crashing Spellnet wasn't that hard. I deleted their information and then ran a virus that fried the system," Claire said.

"Well, if that's what Iz wanted you to do, she can't be mad at you for doing it. I'm sure you'll be fine," Emilia said, rubbing Claire's back.

"That's not the part where I get sent home." Claire opened her vividly pink laptop and started the process of opening her encrypted files. "Before I deleted the files, I may have reallocated some of them to my computer."

"Reallocated?" Emilia raised her left eyebrow.

"You know you look a lot like Aunt Iz when you do that?"

Emilia's eyebrow climbed even higher.

"Fine, I stole some information. It seemed a pity to throw *all* of it out when we could use it to do some actual good in this cold, hard world."

"What exactly did you take, Claire?" Emilia tried to keep her tone level.

"A few things. The information on Wizard-owned patents, the Spellnet Satellite codes, and the registered Witch and Wizard database."

"Claire, that information is confidential."

"I'm not going to go flashing it around if that's what you're worried about. And besides, you should be grateful. I found something I think will interest you. Unless, of course, you don't want your present?" She paused. When Emilia didn't respond, Claire continued. "I didn't think so. I went through the files of registered Witches and Wizards. I found your father's file." Claire clicked on a folder labeled *Emile LeFay*. "And I think"—Claire took a deep breath—"I found your mother."

Emilia froze. "Claire, LeFay didn't tell me her name. Iz doesn't know who she was. She tried to find her. She asked MAGI for help."

"Iz didn't have free range over the files. And they weren't completely computerized then. All I had to do was enter disappearances around your birthday. It was a lot easier than I thought it would be. I had plans for all kinds of ways to search for her. She was one of only five reported missing around that time, and she was the only girl." Claire clicked open a file.

A photo labeled *Rosalie Wilde* stared out from the screen. The girl in the picture had long, black hair that hung in heavy curls. Her features were smaller than Emilia's, and her eyes were blue instead of grey, but Emilia knew in an instant that Claire was right. Rosalie Wilde was her mother.

"What does it say about her?" Emilia brushed the tears away from her eyes so they wouldn't blur her view of the screen.

"She was a runaway. She and LeFay were apprenticed in the same house. He graduated, and she ran away three weeks later. Her family asked MAGI to help find her. It looks like MAGI put out a few inquiries." Claire scrolled down to a scanned document with dates and contacts, a record of MAGI's failed attempts to locate Rosalie. "They didn't do much until after there were a few murders reported near the Graylock Preserve."

Dark mountains and flames flooded Emilia's mind.

"Over the course of five months, two of the wizards who were listed as missing at the same time as your mother were found dead, along with five humans. A couple matching LeFay's and Rosalie's descriptions were seen in the area. That's when MAGI really started looking for her."

"Because they thought she was a murderer," Emilia said dryly.

"There's no evidence I can find that ties her to any of the deaths, and both of the wizards' deaths were ruled accidental."

"LeFay is a murderer, and if Rosalie was there, she must have been helping him." Emilia pushed herself off the bed and started pacing. She never should have let Claire come in. Being alone was better than this.

"But she left, Em."

Emilia's neck tensed. "Please don't call me that."

That was what Dexter had called her. She hated the sound of it now.

"Okay, Emilia. I won't," Claire said quietly. She was silent for a minute while Emilia continued to pace the room. "These records say Rosalie left Graylock right after the first bodies were found. MAGI started looking for LeFay and Rosalie. LeFay never surfaced, but there were sightings of Rosalie.

"She was seen in a small town in Massachusetts two months

after she disappeared from the preserve. Then nothing for about six months. After that, she was seen in California, New York City, and the last sighting was in Maine five months after you were born." Claire closed the laptop and watched Emilia's progress back and forth across the room.

"Thank you, Claire," Emilia said, not looking at her. "Thank you for finding this for me."

"Every time your mom was seen, there was no sign of LeFay. And they were looking for him, too. I think she really did leave him. Emilia, if her birthday on file is right, she was only eighteen when she had you. But she left LeFay. She ran away, alone and pregnant." Claire stood and hugged Emilia, stopping her from moving. "I think she got scared of him and ran. I think she was trying to protect you. If she thought what he was doing was right, she would have stayed with him. It would have been easier. I really think she loved you. I wanted you to know."

Emilia wrapped her arms around Claire. "Thanks, Claire. It's nice to know her name."

"No problem," Claire said, brushing the tears from Emilia's cheek, "and I made a whole file about her. It kind of made me feel like a creeper, but when you want it, let me know." Claire picked up her laptop and started for the door.

"What happened to her?" Emilia asked, not sure she wanted an answer.

"The MAGI trail ends in Maine. But I can work on finding out more if you want."

"That would be great." Emilia nodded. "But don't tell anyone."

"Our secret." Claire smiled and slipped into the dark hall, closing the door silently behind her.

Emilia flopped down onto the bed. Rosalie Wilde. Scared, eighteen, mother? Or evil, wizard supremacist, murderer? She pulled her pillow over her face. All she could see was the smiling, blue-eyed girl, only a year older than herself. But LeFay was eighteen once, too.

3

LESSONS WITH MOLLY

"The thing you've got to remember is to stay covered," Molly said, her voice clipped and tense as she led Jacob, Emilia, Connor, and Claire deeper into the woods behind the house. "You can stand in a field shouting spells as much as you want, but when it comes down to fighting for your life, you want to keep your body covered."

They were far enough into the trees that the house could no longer be seen. Jacob's chest tightened. He clenched his fists as he forced himself to walk farther from the house. From safety. He glanced behind at Emilia. She was pale, and though the day was cool, sweat glistened on her forehead. Molly didn't know Emilia and Jacob had fought in the woods. Molly didn't know Jacob had killed to protect Emilia.

Emilia walked faster, catching up to Jacob. She touched his arm and opened her mouth as though to speak before shaking her head and falling behind.

Molly had stopped walking and was talking again.

"First things first. I want you to give yourselves a bit of protection." Molly had never taught any lessons at the Mansion

House. It seemed strange that it was now her job to teach them to fight.

It should have been Samuel, Jacob thought.

"All of you know how to do a shield spell. Let's see it," Molly ordered.

There was a murmured chorus of *"primurgo."*

The air around Jacob shimmered as his spell surrounded him.

"Fulguratus." Molly formed a glowing bolt of lightning in her hand, which she threw at Jacob. The bolt bounced harmlessly off his shield. "Well done, Jacob."

Molly threw another bolt at Emilia and one at Connor.

"Fulguratus." Molly tossed a bolt at Claire.

"Ouch." Claire rubbed her arm where the bolt hit.

"If you would focus, it wouldn't hurt," Molly said. She didn't sound like the Molly who made breakfast every morning and always had treats hidden in the kitchen. She had changed. They all had.

"Talismans down here, please." Molly pointed to the base of a tree near her feet. "We don't want any of your spells getting too strong."

Emilia slid the necklace with the sapphire pendant over her head and laid it in the grass. Jacob gripped his wand. He didn't want to be without it, not even for a moment. Emilia caught his eye, her brow furrowed. Jacob placed his wand next to the necklace. Molly wouldn't hurt them.

Claire pulled off her silver ring, took Connor's wand from him, and slid the ring onto it.

"What?" Claire asked when Connor glared at her. "It'll be safer that way."

"Now," Molly said loudly, keeping Connor from arguing with Claire, "I want each of you to take ten seconds to run into the trees. Your goal is to make it back to the house. If you get hit, by me or by each other, consider yourself dead. Keep down, keep covered, and get to the house."

Connor began to ask a question.

"Go!" Molly shouted. "Ten, nine, eight…"

Jacob followed Emilia as she took off running through the trees. Out of the corner of his eye, he saw Connor bolt down the path to the house. It was a mistake, the path was too open.

"*Provis!*" Molly shouted, and Connor hit the ground with a yelp.

"Hey!" Connor's indignant shout carried over the sounds of Jacob crashing through branches.

Jacob stayed close behind Emilia as she wound through the trees. His instincts screamed to protect her, even if it was only from Molly.

"*Chrystilla!*" Golden sparks hit a tree to Emilia's left.

"*Verto!*" Jacob shouted over his shoulder.

The ground in front of Emilia began to shake. "Emilia, watch out!"

She dodged to the side as a crack formed in the earth.

Jacob was too busy watching Emilia leap to safety to notice the ground splitting under his own feet. His toes caught in a crevice, and he fell with a grunt. Before he could push himself up, Emilia had grabbed his hand, yanking him to his feet. The instant their hands met, he felt Emilia's heart beating, her adrenaline pumping.

"*Gelethra!*" Molly's shout cut through the trees.

The air around Jacob's feet shimmered, and as he moved to take another step, his foot stuck to the ground as though trapped by mud. Jacob waved his free arm wildly, desperately trying to regain his balance, before he tipped over, releasing his grip on Emilia as he fell again. Pain shot through his hand as a rock sliced his palm.

"*Macolia!*" Molly shouted.

Out of the corner of his eye, Jacob saw leaves swirl in front of Claire, who glanced back at Molly as the leaves formed a solid wall, blocking her path. Claire rammed into the wall at full speed.

The leaves quivered, and a *boom* like a large drum nearly covered her squeal as she tumbled to the ground.

"Really?" Claire groaned, holding her shoulder and lying in the dirt.

Jacob grabbed Emilia's hand and pulled her farther into the trees, cutting a wide angle back to the house. His hand was slick with blood and Emilia's grip tightened as she almost slipped away.

"*Perectus!*" The sound of a tree cracking echoed behind them.

Emilia screamed, stopping as though frozen by the spell.

"Emilia." Jacob turned to her, but she didn't stop screaming. She fell to the ground, covering her head, hiding from some unseen horror.

"Emi." Jacob knelt beside her and wrapped his arms around her.

"No!" Emilia lashed out, hitting and scratching him.

Her nails dug into Jacob's face as she knocked him to the ground.

"Please don't hurt him," Emilia sobbed, covering her ears.

Jacob gathered her into his arms, holding her to his chest.

"You're fine. It's okay. You're okay," Jacob murmured. "I won't let anyone hurt you."

Emilia gasped, struggling to breathe through her tears.

"You're safe," Jacob whispered.

"Emilia?" Claire stood next to them, her face white with fear.

"She's fine," Jacob said, not loosening his hold on Emilia.

Emilia pushed away from him, her gaze searching the trees before finding Jacob's face. "I'm sorry." Emilia stood up and stumbled away from him.

"Emilia," Molly said. "You should take a minute, and then we can continue."

"No." Emilia shook her head. "I can't do this." She tore through the trees and back to the house.

Jacob turned and walked back through the woods to where they had left their talismans, fighting the urge to follow Emilia. She wouldn't want him with her.

"I don't think Emilia should come back out here," Connor said, glancing over his shoulder at Molly.

Jacob didn't say anything. He picked up Emilia's necklace and slipped it into his pocket.

Connor slid Claire's ring off his wand and tossed the silver band back to her.

"She has to come back out to train," Molly said with a harsh authority that seemed strange coming from her.

"Not in the woods," Jacob said quietly, not looking at the rest of the group. "She shouldn't come back out here."

"She doesn't have a choice," Molly said. "Do you think the Dragons are going the let her choose where she wants to fight? Do you think they'll let her find a nice place before they try to kill her?"

"I think she already knows what it's like to fight the Dragons," Jacob said, staring into Molly's eyes.

Molly glared back at him. Jacob could tell she was angry, but he didn't flinch.

"Aunt Molly," Connor said. "Maybe we should practice by the house."

"You will practice where I tell you to, Connor Wright," Molly said, rounding on Connor. "Your parents are still living on the High Peaks Preserve. Just because they haven't been set upon by Dragons yet doesn't mean it will stay that way. If your parents are attacked, if they are captured, you need to be able to defend your family. You have to be able to protect yourself."

Molly was telling a fourteen-year-old he needed to be able to protect his family. The world was falling apart.

"*Pelluere.*" Jacob clenched his teeth as the sting of healing seared his palm.

Molly took Jacob's hand, examining the place where the rock had pierced it. "Well done, Jacob. Claire, heal Jacob's cheek. You need the practice."

Claire didn't seem nervous as she held her palm out toward Jacob's face. Jacob tried to look calm as well. "*Pelluere.*"

Jacob felt the warmth of Claire's spell before the stinging set in as his skin knit back together. He resisted the temptation to touch his face to make sure everything was still in the right place.

"You look good." Claire smiled at him.

Molly walked over and inspected Claire's work. "Nicely done."

Claire smiled and bounced a bit at the praise.

"We'll meet again tomorrow. Tidy up this mess before you come back to the house. I'll go get dinner ready." She walked back through the trees.

"She's a bit creepy these days," Claire said. "I know you said she had fought before, but I didn't know she could be like this." Claire gestured to the cracks in the ground and the fallen trees.

"It is weird," Connor agreed. "*Ramono.*" The tree branch that lay at Connor's feet flew back up through the air and reattached itself seamlessly to the tree.

"Where exactly did Molly fight?" Jacob asked.

"*Tellura,*" Claire said. The ground shook under their feet as a crack in the dirt rumbled back together.

"At the High Peaks Preserve," Connor said. "The settlement my parents are with. They were attacked. Travelers, wizards without a Clan, and centaurs. They all wanted the land my family was on, so my family defended it. They had to fight on and off for years. I don't know much about it, but I know it got pretty bad sometimes. That's why my parents sent me here."

"Right," Jacob said. "*Prasinuro.*" The flower stems at their feet straightened, and the singe marks on the trees disappeared.

"Let's go," Claire said, threading her arm through Jacob's.

"I'll catch up in a bit." Jacob took a step back, disconnecting his arm from Claire's. "I want to take a walk."

"But—" Claire began to protest, but Connor took her hand and dragged her toward the house.

Jacob headed right, cutting sideways into the woods. He needed a minute to think away from the house. Away from everyone. In a few minutes, he found a clearing with a bench and one beautiful tree.

Jacob lay in the grass, staring up through the branches of his tree—the tree he had healed not even half a year before. It seemed like forever ago that he had lain in this exact same place and the tree had dropped a stick on his face. The stick that had become his wand.

Jacob twirled his wand through his fingers like a baton. It was strange how much a piece of wood could do. At the beginning, it was just a stick. Something to prove to himself that he was a wizard. That he, Jacob Evans, was meant to be a part of the magical world. But now, with all the hours of practice and all the magic he had done, the wand had become a part of him. After using it to fight for his and Emilia's lives, he felt naked and vulnerable without it.

The smooth surface of the wand glinted in the sunlight. There had been one spell Jacob had done without his wand. Emilia was trapped, and there was no escape. Bile rose in his throat as he remembered the heat that had burst through his skin.

Shrieks of pain and fear ripping from the mouths of the Dragons that had pinned Emilia down. Screams echoing through the woods. Fire turning the trees black but leaving Jacob and Emilia alive. Jacob sat up and forced himself to breathe, swallowing the sour in his mouth.

He should have died doing that spell. Using that much magic without a talisman to draw the energy away from his body was suicide. He'd known it and had done the spell anyway. Anything to save Emilia, to keep her from being taken back to the caves. Yet he had survived. He had survived, and the Dragons had died.

But he didn't know how. Jacob looked at his hands—one streaked in gold, the other plain. Nothing on either of them showed he was special, that he could survive the impossible. Nothing marked him as a killer either.

He felt a pull in his chest.

Emilia.

She was angry, furious. Jacob resisted the temptation to run to the house. She didn't want to be bound to him. His responding to her moods only made it worse. Every time he felt his heart lurch with a feeling that was not his own, Jacob wanted to run to her, to hold her and tell her everything was all right. But it wasn't all right, and eavesdropping on her feelings wasn't making anything better, even if he couldn't help it.

The rage in Jacob's chest didn't subside. He sighed and stood, patting his tree goodbye before heading inside. He found Connor and Claire staring up at the ceiling.

"What are you doing?" Jacob asked, following their gaze, half-expecting to see a fairy flying above them. But the hallway ceiling looked normal. Not a flying magical thing in sight.

"Wait for it," Claire said, not moving. A few seconds later, a horrible *crash* echoed from above.

Jacob started toward the stairs, but Connor grabbed his arm.

"I wouldn't if I were you," Connor warned.

"But someone could be hurt."

"She's fine," Claire said serenely. "It's probably good therapy. Getting out aggressions or something."

"What?" Jacob looked back at the ceiling as the sound of shattering glass floated down the stairs.

"Emilia's trashing Dexter's room," Connor said, looking apologetic for mentioning Dexter's name. "I ran upstairs when I heard the first crash." Connor glanced at Claire.

"Neither of us is brave enough to go in there," Claire said. "She's a little scary right now."

Jacob turned back to the stairs. A shriek came from above.

"I'll go check on her," Jacob said.

"Godspeed, and gird your loins!" Claire called after him.

4

DESTRUCTIVE TENDENCIES

*J*acob climbed the grand staircase and crossed the hall to the small servants' stairs that led up to the top floor where the boys slept. The higher he got, the more detail he could hear in the chaos. *Thumps* that sounded like drawers being tossed from a dresser shook the floor as he reached the door to Dexter's room.

The door was open, and the room had been ransacked. Every drawer had been emptied. All the clothes had been pulled from the closet. The mattress had been flipped off the bed and was lying next to the remains of a lamp. Jacob had never seen the inside of this room while Dexter had lived in it, but he recognized the belongings as Dexter's.

The clothes were expensive. The speakers that Dexter had played his music through were in pieces on the floor. A shining leather bag and a smashed gold watch joined the rest of the debris. And in the middle of it all stood Emilia.

She turned to look at Jacob, a stack of books in her hands.

"You okay?" he asked, stepping lightly as something crunched under his feet.

"Fine," Emilia said. "Why?"

Jacob gestured to the pile at his feet.

"Oh." Emilia pasted a smile on her face, the one that said she was lying, pretending to be all right. "I was looking for something."

Jacob said nothing. They stood staring at each other.

"Would you like help?" Jacob finally asked. "I'm sure I could find a few things in here I'd like to break, too." He picked a photo of Dexter and Emilia up off the floor. Dexter's arm was draped casually around Emilia's shoulder, and she was beaming. They looked natural together, as if they were meant to be like that, frozen in that picture forever.

Emilia pulled the picture from Jacob's hand. "*Inexuro.*" She dropped the burning photo into the trashcan. "That's not the right picture." Emilia started shaking out each of the books.

"Which picture are you looking for?" Jacob asked, afraid to hear the answer. Was there a picture of her and Dexter she wanted to keep?

"It doesn't matter." Emilia sat on the bare box spring. "I don't think it's here."

"What's not here?" Jacob asked, not moving, unsure if he should sit near her.

"When we were there," Emilia said, "LeFay, the Pendragon— he said he had seen a picture of me. That's how he knew—" She stopped. Jacob understood the words she could not say. *He knew I was his daughter.*

"It could have been any picture." Jacob took a step closer to her. This was the first time she had mentioned Graylock since the night they got back. Talking about the caves had been silently forbidden.

"Dexter took the picture, he must have. The Pendragon said he saw me with my necklace."

Jacob pulled the sapphire pendant from his pocket and handed it to her.

Emilia held it in her palm. The stone sparkled even in the dim light of the room. Silver veins ran across its teardrop surface.

"You brought this back to me when you came to live with us. Dexter must have taken the picture the Pendragon saw. I didn't leave the Mansion House once you got here. It couldn't have been anyone else. I want to see it. I want to see what Dexter gave him. I need to." Emilia looked at Jacob, her eyes begging him to understand. "I don't know where else to look."

"We can search together," Jacob said, picking up a drawer and shaking it, making sure there was nothing left stuck inside.

"It was probably on his phone. He was always taking pictures of me with his stupid phone." Emilia moved to kneel on the floor.

"*Ablutere*," Jacob said quickly, and the broken glass slid away from Emilia and into a pile next to the door. Jacob picked up a stack of papers that looked to have been on the nightstand.

"Thanks," Emilia murmured. "I just want to know why. Did the Dragons ask him for a picture of me?"

Jacob's heart sank as realization flooded him. "It was me. If a picture got sent to the Pendragon, he must have wanted a picture of me. They were trying to blame everything on me. Remember, they wanted everyone to believe I had destroyed my school on purpose."

"We all have destructive tendencies." Emilia made a sweeping gesture to the wreckage that used to be Dexter's room.

"But Aunt Iz told me they were trying to use me as an example of the kind of damage wizards should be doing in order for Magickind to gain power. If the Dragons wanted me on their side, Dexter would have been the one to gather information for them. I was with you every second I could be. If he took a picture of me, you would have been in it."

Being locked in a stone box, tortured, seeing Domina's dead eyes. Rescuing Emilia and being bound to her. He had thought it was the Dragons' doing. Another unstoppable extension of their evil. But it wasn't. It was his, Jacob's, fault. If he hadn't come to the Mansion House, if he hadn't tried so hard to win Emilia from Dexter, the Pendragon would never have found Emilia. He wouldn't have kidnapped her off the streets of New York. And Graylock would never have happened.

His magic at his school. He had started it all.

Emilia laced her fingers through his. He felt her touch calming him, and for the first time she didn't pull away.

"It's not your fault. If Dexter was giving his father and the Pendragon information, they would have figured out who I am eventually. And Dexter wanted me to be with the Dragons so I could be on *the winning side* of this fight. He would have asked the Dragons to take me to protect me, and the Pendragon would have figured it out then." Emilia rested her head on Jacob's shoulder. "And maybe you wouldn't have been able to save me."

"I would have found a way." Jacob wrapped his arms around her, savoring the feeling of her being safe. For the first time in months, he felt like he could breathe. "I will always find a way."

"I know." Emilia brushed the shaggy blond hair away from Jacob's eyes. "I've missed you."

"I missed you, too." Jacob took a breath. She was so close, there in his arms.

"We should get out of here." Emilia stepped back suddenly. "If I spend any more time in here, I'll be tempted to light the whole room on fire."

"Iz wouldn't like that." Jacob didn't look at Emilia as they left the room.

"Forget Aunt Iz," Emilia said with a tired laugh. "This room is right above Claire's. I don't even want to think about how angry she would be if I caught her closet on fire."

Jacob shuddered at the thought of little blond Claire trying to murder both of them for damaging her precious clothing. He didn't like the idea of a truly angry Claire.

"See you at dinner," Emilia said as she headed down the stairs.

Jacob crossed the hall and threw himself onto his bed. He had talked to Emilia. They had had an actual conversation, which was more than they had managed since they had been tethered. And she didn't blame him. Not for being kidnapped, or being tethered to him, or even Samuel and Larkin being gone. Jacob took a deep breath, willing tears not to form in his eyes.

Aunt Iz had said she thought Samuel might still be alive. If they could find Samuel and Larkin, if they could bring them home, maybe things would be all right.

Jacob rolled over and buried his face in his soft, green comforter. Saving Samuel and Larkin would be wonderful. Having them alive and home where they belonged, it would help them all. But it wouldn't undo the tethering. Nothing could do that but death.

5

BEHIND GLASS

*E*milia sat on the veranda, curled up in a blanket. She gazed through the trees. The first hints of gold touched their leaves. They looked peaceful. She knew somewhere out in the woods centaurs patrolled the borders of the property. And beyond the centaurs, the *fortaceria*, the shield spell that surrounded the Mansion House, would block any who dared to attack.

Iz had done everything she could to protect the house. Communication with the outside had been cut off. Emilia smirked as she remembered Claire's tantrum when the internet had been disconnected. There were spells and shields protecting them, but it still felt strange to sit alone outside the house. Exposed.

Could someone be watching the house now? The Pendragon —she shuddered, trying to keep from thinking the words *my father*—was still out there. It had been months since he had tried to burn her and Jacob to death in the woods. He hadn't tried to contact, or kidnap, or kill her since. And that scared her. How did someone go from trying to murder you to leaving you alone completely?

He would come for her, that much she knew. But when? And how many more people she loved would he hurt to get to her?

"Emilia," Connor called as he opened the door to the veranda, "Ms. Gray wants all of us in the dining room, right now."

Emilia stood and followed him inside. The air in the house felt different. If fear had a scent, it was here.

When they got to the dining room, the whole family was already seated. Professor Eames had tracks of tears running down his face, Molly was even paler than usual, and Iz didn't look at Emilia as she entered the room.

Emilia moved to take her seat next to Claire, but something made her stop. She picked up her chair and put it next to Jacob's. Whatever was wrong, if it had to do with the Pendragon, then it was her and Jacob he was after, even more than Aunt Iz.

Claire raised an eyebrow and grinned at Emilia.

"I am sorry to have to call all of you here," Aunt Iz said. "I received a skry from Rendell of the Bonforte Clan."

Emilia gripped the arms of her chair. The Bonforte Clan was way down south. They were centered in Louisiana. What could have happened so far away?

"Rendell hadn't heard from Olivia for a few days. He got worried and went to her estate. It had been destroyed," Iz said, her voice flat.

"What do you mean *destroyed*?" Jacob sat forward in his seat. "Did they burn it?"

"It appears the Dragons released Nandi from the Bois Noir Confine," Iz said.

Emilia shuddered along with everyone else but Jacob.

"What's a Nandi?" Jacob asked, looking from Iz to Professor Eames.

"Nandi are more like hyenas than any other normal beast," Professor Eames answered. "Fanged, blood thirsty, and extraordinarily strong, they're confined in one of the Bonforte Clan

Preserves, far out of reach of humans. Nandi are vicious creatures and cannot be harmed by most spells. If they attacked without warning, there would have been little hope of the Bonfortes defending themselves. And it appears the Nandi came in the night."

"How did they get to Miss Olivia's house?" Claire asked. "If they were supposed to be locked up?"

"We are still working on that," Aunt Iz said. "Other members of the Bonforte Clan are looking into it."

"Was anyone else at the estate?" Emilia asked, trying to push the images of gnashing teeth and blood-soaked fur from her mind.

"A few family members, guards"—Aunt Iz paused—"and a few students."

"Did anyone survive?" Connor asked.

"No," Iz said, her voice shaking for the first time. "There were no survivors or Nandi left when Rendell got to the estate."

"Are they trying to find the Nandi?" Claire looked over her shoulder at the door as though expecting a herd of snarling beasts to come bursting into the house.

Emilia resisted the urge to look as well.

"They are." Iz nodded. "We are sending some of our Clan to join the search."

"My dad?" Connor asked.

"Yes, he is with the group," Molly said.

"I want to go help him." Connor stood up. "If my dad is out there, I should be, too."

"Your father wants you here where you're safe," Molly said.

"Are we safe?" Claire reached out and pulled Connor back to his seat.

Aunt Iz didn't answer.

"We're as safe as we can be, Claire." Emilia tried to muster a smile. "We'll be fine."

Emilia reached over and took Jacob's hand, using his touch to keep herself from slipping into the panic that pounded in her chest. Jacob squeezed her hand, and she felt a little calmer.

"I liked Miss Olivia," Claire said softly. "She was nice to me when she came to help us look for you."

"She was a wonderful woman," Professor Eames said. "She will be missed."

Molly stood and left the room. Connor followed her out.

Sometimes Emilia forgot they were a part of a family away from the Grays. The danger went beyond the people in this house. Even the humans were threatened, though they didn't know it.

Iz left, and the professor followed, shuffling out of the room, looking every bit the elderly man he was.

As soon as he was gone, Claire turned to Emilia. "Do you really think Connor's family should stay out in the woods? Shouldn't we make them come here?"

"Aunt Iz will figure it out," Emilia said.

"But we'll all be together?" Claire's bottom lip trembled.

"We'll do whatever we have to to stay safe," Emilia said.

Claire stood and hugged Jacob and Emilia, banging their heads together, before running out of the room.

Jacob watched Claire leave. "Do you think Iz will keep us all here?" he said as Claire's footsteps pounded up the stairs.

"She'll do whatever it takes to keep us alive." Emilia covered her face with her hands, blocking out the light of the room. "And if she thinks we'll be better off away from the Mansion House, away from her, she'll make us go."

"They would all be safer without us," Jacob muttered.

Emilia dropped her hands. She had known that was true but hadn't expected Jacob to say it.

"Claire, Connor, all of them would be safer far away from the two of us." Jacob stood, as though ready to run away. "What do we do?"

His eyes were wide and desperate. This was his family, too.

Emilia wanted to hold him, to tell him everything would be all right. But that was a lie. There could be Nandi in the woods around the house right now.

"We have to stay here. We have to make sure everyone is protected." Emilia turned and left the room. They had to stay with the family.

For now.

~

*I*t was drizzling and cold. The wind whipped through her hair. The night was dark with only the streetlamps to light the way. Emilia walked down the path. Cages lined both sides, but Emilia was drawn to a large window up ahead.

She peered down into the enclosure expecting to see a lion, but instead she saw a centaur picking food out of a dog bowl and another batting at a ball.

Suddenly the sun was blazing, and children were banging on the glass, tormenting the centaurs who hid behind the boulders in their pen. Emilia tried to claw through the glass, desperate to free the centaurs, but she couldn't break through.

She ran, pushing her way through the crowd to find another way in, but every time she turned a corner, another magical species was locked up—mermaids in tanks, fauns in a cage. She ran through an entire building with fairies in terrariums along the walls. At the end of the fairy house, she burst through a door and ran into a circus ring.

A spotlight blinded her. She looked down at her body and realized she was wearing a skimpy witch costume. The crowd jeered. She turned to go back the way she'd come, but the door was gone. Dexter's voice resonated through the circus tent.

"Ladies and gentlemen, up next we have our very own Emilia Gray, the Wicked Witch and Dragon Tamer."

Emilia looked at her hand, which now held a long, black leather whip. Flames lashed at her face from across the ring as an enormous dragon crept toward her, spitting fire and gnashing its teeth. Emilia tried to run away, but no matter how fast she ran, she could not escape the dragon. The ground disappeared beneath her, and she was running on a tight rope. She looked down and heard the crowd gasp as she slipped from the rope and fell into the dragon's waiting mouth.

$\approx$

*E*milia sat up in bed, trying to stifle her own scream. She pulled a pillow to her chest, shaking and drenched in her own sweat.

6

SAFER APART

*J*acob woke with a gasp. A fear that had nothing to do with himself gripped his lungs. He looked wildly around the room, searching for whatever had frightened him out of his sleep, but his room was empty. The only noise, his own ragged breaths. He felt another pang and knew what was wrong. "Emilia," he gasped as he ran for the door.

He didn't bother trying to be quiet as he tore through the house. Emilia's door swung open before Jacob could reach for the knob. He ran into the room, prepared to fight whoever was harming Emilia. He saw Emilia on the bed, tears streaming down her face, before swinging around, searching for her attacker. But no one was there.

"Emi." Jacob went to the bed and pulled her into his arms. "You're shaking."

"I'm fine." Emilia pushed herself away from Jacob's embrace and wiped the tears from her cheeks.

"No you're not. You were terrified. I felt it from my room. It woke me up. What happened?"

"I'm sorry I bothered you." Emilia picked up her brush and tore it through her long black hair.

"I'm not. I'm glad you woke me up. If you're scared, I want to be here." Jacob paused. "Was it a nightmare?"

Emilia brushed her hair faster.

Jacob reached over and gently took Emilia's hand, halting it mid-stroke.

"Am I weak?" Emilia whispered. "Am I contaminated, or broken, or crazy? I'm a mess. I'm scared all the time. Scared of what's happening out there and scared they might come after us here. I freaked out in the woods with Molly. I'm terrified of what they might be doing to Larkin and Samuel. If they're even alive. And I don't know if I should hope they aren't." Fresh tears streamed down Emilia's cheeks. "I can't sleep. My magic isn't working right."

"I'm scared, too," Jacob said quietly. "I'm scared of what's coming, of what might happen to this family, to you."

"But you sleep through the night—"

"Not always." Jacob shook his head. "And after what they put you through—"

"Put *me* through? They locked me in a room. What that evil woman did to you, I can't even imagine."

"It doesn't matter," Jacob said. "Domina can't hurt anyone anymore."

Because I killed her.

"And then finally when you escaped, you tried to save me and ended up being tethered to me," Emilia continued, her voice rising into a shriek.

"I don't mind." Jacob stared at the purple flowers on the rug, trying to keep his voice steady. "It doesn't matter."

"It doesn't matter? You saved me, and in return you ended up bound to me for the rest of our lives."

"Is that so bad?" Jacob's hands were the ones shaking now. "Is it so bad to be tethered to me? I mean, I know it's not what either of us would have chosen, but you had to be joined to someone..." What if she would rather have been joined to Dexter?

Emilia took Jacob's hands in hers. The pale golden streak on both of their left palms began to shimmer. "I'm glad it's you. You're my best friend. I trust you. If you hadn't saved me, I would be trapped with those murderers and tethered to Dexter. But you, if you hadn't come for me, you would be free."

"If I hadn't come for you, I would have lost the person who means the most to me in the whole world." Jacob pressed his forehead to Emilia's. "We're in this together now, Emi."

"Together." She lay down at the head of her bed, curling up like a wounded kitten. Jacob lay at the foot of the bed, wishing he could reach across the foot of space between them. Wanting to hold Emilia close so he would know she was safe.

"*Perluxeo,*" Emilia murmured, and the room went black.

The only light left in the room was the golden gleam across both of their palms.

~

*T*he next morning, the students sat in the library, trying to focus on their work. None of them dared mention Iz and the professor hadn't been seen all morning.

Jacob had heard their voices coming out of Iz's study on his way to breakfast. It sounded like they were arguing about something. He had never even heard rumor of the professor and Iz fighting before.

Claire tapped her pencil on the desk, and from the daggers Connor glared at her, it wouldn't be long before there was a fight in the library as well. Footsteps carried down the hall. Every head snapped toward the door as Iz appeared.

"Claire," Iz said, "I need to speak to you in my study."

"I didn't do it," Claire blurted immediately.

"I didn't say you did anything wrong, Claire. I said I needed to speak with you." The smile that should have touched Iz's eyes with such an exchange was missing.

Claire stood silently and followed Iz down the hall to her office.

Jacob glanced at Emilia, but she shook her head. She didn't know what was going on either. Jacob went back to his reading.

PRIMURGO MOTUS

A moving shield spell is an intricate piece of magic that is rarely mastered. The need to block another wizard's spell while allowing your own to penetrate the shield is complex. That consideration coupled with the necessary movement of the shield with the casting wizard creates an unreliable—

A shriek echoed down the hall. Footsteps pounded toward them.

"I won't," Claire screamed.

Jacob stood, knocking his chair to the ground as Claire hurtled around the corner and ran to Emilia's side.

"Claire," Emilia said, standing.

"She wants to send me away." Claire clung to Emilia. "She wants to take away my magic and send me away!"

"What?" Emilia looked at Aunt Iz, who stood in the doorway.

"Emilia, don't let her do it!" Claire screeched, hiding behind Emilia.

Connor moved to stand next to Claire.

"I am not taking away your magic," Aunt Iz said, barely loudly enough to be heard over Claire's sobs. "I am going to bind your powers temporarily."

"Why?" Connor asked. "She needs her magic. We all do. If the Mansion House is attacked—"

"Then none of you will be here," Iz said. "The decision has been made. The four of you are to leave here today. Jacob and Emilia will be going to stay with some friends of the family. They are well equipped to protect you. Connor, you will join them until your parents find another place for you. Claire is going to be returning to her family."

"No!" Claire shouted.

"And, since they are humans and Claire is not fully trained, we will temporarily bind her powers. When all of this is over, I promise we will come and get you. We will unbind your magic, and you can continue your education. This is the safest thing for you."

"I won't let you!" Claire sobbed.

"You need to go back to your family." Iz's voice caught in her throat.

"This is my family." Tears coursed down Claire's cheeks. "I don't even know my parents. I have a sister I've only ever seen at Christmas."

"Then maybe it's time you get to know them," Emilia said, tipping Claire's chin up to meet her eyes. "Get to know your little sister."

"I belong here." Claire pulled away from Emilia. "I'm a witch. I belong with you."

"Claire—" Aunt Iz started.

"I won't sit in Connecticut waiting to see if the Dragons take over." Claire shook her head, sending her bright blond hair flying wildly. "If you send me home, I'll tell everyone I can all about witches and the Dragons. I'll make sure everyone knows that MAGI had satellites watching them, and that the Council of Elders failed."

"Claire, I know you're upset, but do you really think people would believe a twelve-year-old girl?" Iz asked. "And even trying to explain the magical world to humans would end in your powers being bound forever."

"Who would bind them? The Council? The Council fell. You? Would you really do that to me? Would you actually make me a *Demadais*? Because it would be your fault!" Claire shouted. "And people may not believe a twelve-year-old, but you would be amazed at what a good hacker can do."

"Claire, you can't," Iz snapped. "If the humans knew—"

"Then they would come after my family. They would come

after you, and Molly, and the professor," Claire spat. "I would never hurt anyone in this house. And I won't leave them, either."

Connor reached out and took Claire's hand.

"She's as much a part of this family as I am," Connor said. "There is no safe place for any of us anymore, Ms. Gray."

Claire held tightly onto Connor. "I'll go with Emilia, Connor, and Jacob. This family is my home. If they have to hide, I'll hide with them. I'll fight with them. I don't care. We're staying together."

Aunt Iz shook her head. "The professor thought this would happen. All I want is for you to be safe." Iz sighed. "You can stay with the others, Claire."

"I can keep my magic?" Claire asked, still clutching Connor's hand.

"Yes."

"And you won't send me back to my parents?"

"Not yet." Aunt Iz shook her head. "Your having been with the family so long will put you in danger no matter where you are."

"Thank you!" Claire bounded across the room and threw herself at Iz, burying her face in Iz's shoulder for a moment.

"What are you going to tell my parents?" Claire looked up at Iz, brushing the tears from her cheeks with the back of her hand.

"Nothing. We haven't told them about the Dragons. We thought it would be safer."

Claire nodded.

"All of you go upstairs and pack. You'll be leaving in a few hours. One bag only, Claire." Aunt Iz caught Claire's arm as she began to run for the stairs. "And pack for cold weather. And camping."

Jacob followed Emilia upstairs. "Where do you think she's sending us?" he asked once Claire and Connor were out of earshot.

"I'm not sure," Emilia said as she went into her room. The door closed behind Jacob with a soft *click*. "Sounds like one of the preserves. But then we might as well go to Connor's mother."

Emilia pulled a duffle bag from under her bed.

"Do you think she should have sent Claire to her parents?" Jacob asked. "Would she be safer?"

Emilia turned away from Jacob and started ripping things violently out of her drawers, tossing selected items onto the bed.

"Emi," Jacob said, picking up a pair of thick jeans that had missed the comforter, "wherever Iz is sending us, we'll be safer."

"You would all be safer if I weren't there." Emilia pulled a pair of hiking boots from the bottom of her closet. "Aunt Iz shouldn't be trying to separate Claire from the family. You and Connor and Claire would be safer if *I* weren't around."

Jacob walked over to Emilia and drew her to his chest. She trembled in his arms. "Miss Olivia was nowhere near you, and the Dragons killed her anyway. None of us are safe."

"But Claire and Connor would be better off far away from me."

"Away from us," Jacob said, looking into Emilia's eyes. His heart skipped, and he stepped away. "Where you go, I go."

"You should pack." Emilia tossed clothes into her bag. "We don't have much time."

"Right." Jacob left Emilia to finish on her own.

He went up the stairs to the servants' wing and into his room. There was a duffle bag open on his bed. Iz must have bought it for him. She had bought him almost everything he owned. Claire had done the shopping, but Iz had paid.

Jacob pulled a small box from the bottom of his closet. It had everything he had brought with him from Fairfield. Everything he had from his life before he found out he was a wizard. Before he joined the Grays.

Jacob opened the box. There were notes from his father, the ones Jim had left on the counter every time he skipped town, and a book his mother had written her name in. They were nothing of value, really, but they were all he had left to link him to his life before magic. Jacob slid the box inside his duffle before tossing clothes on top.

Soon Jacob was downstairs sitting in the kitchen with his duffle bag. Molly was busy at the counter, packing large sacks full of food.

"Do they not have food where Aunt Iz is sending us?" Jacob asked, jokingly.

"Of course they do." Molly didn't look up from the cutting board. "Is it so bad if I want to make sure you children are safe? Can you blame me for wanting to take care of the children I have watched grow up? *Subtorqueo.*" The sandwiches wrapped themselves in plastic before flying into bags. "All I want—" Molly broke off.

"All you want is to keep us safe?" Jacob said.

"I'm not naïve, Jacob." Molly's eyes were red and puffy. "I know that *safe* is not a possibility. What I want is for a part of this family to make it out alive."

Jacob wanted to say something comforting, that they would all survive the Dragons, that the family would be together again soon. But that wasn't true. Things would never be the same. He could lie to Claire to comfort her, but he couldn't lie to Molly. What was the point when she knew the truth?

The last time the family had been separated, it had ended in fire. Jacob's skin tingled as he remembered the heat bursting from within him. The memory of the horrible scent of burning flesh turned his stomach.

"I have to go say goodbye to the professor," Jacob said, managing to stop himself from running back down the hall long enough to give Molly a quick hug around the neck.

7

THE IMPOSSIBLE SPELL

*T*he door to the professor's study was open, and Jacob ran straight in.

"Professor, I need to talk to you," Jacob said before the professor could turn to look at him.

"Jacob, the car will be here any moment," the professor said, his already wrinkled brow furrowed with the stress of the day. "You should be waiting outside."

"I have to ask you a question before I go." Jacob forced himself to say the thing he had been holding onto for months. "When I destroyed my school, when I broke all of those windows, I didn't have a talisman. My magic just exploded out of me, but I didn't get hurt. I was fine."

"Doing magic under extreme circumstances is normal for a new wizard." The professor patted Jacob's hand. "And as we can't ask humans to carry around talismans just in case, the first display of magic is always done without anything to direct the energy away from the body."

"When we were being held in the caves," Jacob pressed on, his mouth dry, "there was a woman. She kept me in a room." The scars on Jacob's cheek and chest burned at the thought of his dark cage, making his heart pound even faster. "I didn't have a talisman, but we fought." Jacob swallowed. Sweat slicked his palms. He didn't want to say the words, but he had to know. "I killed her."

The professor's face turned white as he lowered himself into a chair.

"It was the same thing," Jacob whispered. "I was desperate. I had to get out to save Emilia, and then there was a flash. I felt the magic fly out of me, and then she was dead."

The professor ran a hand across his forehead, as though trying to wipe a horrible image from his mind. "I am sorry this happened to you Jacob. Taking a life, even when you must, is a terrible thing."

"But how did I survive?"

"You are powerful. You were desperate," the professor sighed. "You are the strongest new wizard I have seen in quite some time. You played with the boundaries of how much magic you can do without a talisman and somehow miraculously survived. Your magic was stronger than hers, but do not try magic like that again, Jacob. The next time, if you go even a touch further, it could kill you."

"I did go further." Jacob's voice wavered. He didn't want to see the professor's face when he heard what Jacob had done. "When Emilia and I were escaping Graylock, Emilia was pinned down. She couldn't do anything. Something happened. I did a spell without even thinking. I didn't have my wand. I'd dropped it. But this spell was more than I had ever done before.

"I felt my magic burn. The trees caught fire. I killed the Dragons who had pinned her down. I don't know how I did it, but what if it happens again? What if we get attacked and I hurt Emilia or Connor or Claire?" Jacob drove the image of Claire and Connor burned and dead from his mind.

"Jacob, what you're saying is impossible. You are powerful, and I understand what happened to that woman. It was magic done under extreme pressure. But burning a forest, killing that many people. No one, not even the most powerful wizard, could do a spell like that without a talisman and survive." The professor stood and shuffled forward, taking Jacob's trembling hand in his own withered one. "Perhaps Emilia did a spell you didn't know about."

"It was me," Jacob said, desperate to make the professor understand how dangerous he, Jacob, was. "What if my magic is weird? What if some filter or off switch inside of me is broken and I can't control it?"

"You ready?" Connor popped his head into the study. "The scary guy from MAGI is waiting outside."

"Just one moment more," the professor said, and Connor bounded back down the hall. "Listen to me, Jacob. I don't know what magic you could have done in those woods, and I am not convinced it was your magic that you saw. But if it was, I don't think you need to worry about hurting Connor, Claire, or Emilia.

"If that spell did originate with you, and you had not meant to manipulate it in that way, that means something deep inside you, even deeper than your magic, would not let you hurt Emilia. I know, as the two of you are tethered, a deeper connection is not to be found, but you have a strong heart. You care for Connor and Claire. I don't think you would allow yourself to hurt them, no matter how out of control your magic may seem."

Jacob nodded, finally letting himself breathe. "What about my talisman? I didn't have my wand."

The professor shrugged. "I will see what I can find on incidents like the one you experienced. But Jacob, if you were trapped and Emilia was in danger, perhaps you didn't notice you were holding your wand."

"Jacob, come on!" Claire's shout rang from the front of the house.

"Go, go." The professor shooed Jacob all the way out the front door, following him with wheezy steps. "Go, Jacob. You'll be fine." The professor patted Jacob's arm.

Jacob wanted to say the professor was wrong, that he knew he hadn't had his wand. But the chaos of packing the car surrounded the front of the house, and the whole family would hear.

"I don't know why we can only bring one bag." Claire scowled at the car that waited for them out front. "That trunk is huge."

"You'll be fine, Claire," Jacob said, leaving the professor and walking to the car. He picked up Claire's pink bag and tossed it into the trunk with his own. Emilia and Connor loaded their bags into the trunk as well.

Jacob turned back to the house. Aunt Iz stood to the side, talking to MAGI Stone. He was tall, dark-skinned, and terrifying. Everything from his shining bald head to his enormous muscles made it known that he was not a person to be trifled with.

"Be careful, all of you." Molly gave each of them a tight hug. "Do as you're told, and remember to practice your magic. You must be able to protect each other."

"I will miss you all." Tears slid down the professor's cheek as he said goodbye to each of them, giving Jacob an extra smile of encouragement.

"Take care of Aunt Iz for me," Emilia said as she hugged the elderly man. He looked tiny to Jacob, even next to Emilia.

"We will take care of each other," Aunt Iz said. "And I will be in touch as soon as I can. You had better go. We want to get you there before dark."

"Where?" Claire asked, clinging tightly to Iz.

"Someplace you'll like." Aunt Iz herded them toward the car.

"You take the front." Jacob gestured to Emilia. He looked into the car at Stone, who sat in the driver's seat ready to whisk them away to safety. He had taken Samuel's place.

"No, thanks." Emilia shook her head. "I'll stay in the back and try to keep the kids calm."

"Did you really just call us kids?" Claire planted her hands on her hips. "I take offense to that."

"Leave it, Claire," Connor said, sliding into the middle back seat.

"Fine," Claire said as she climbed in after Connor, "if you won't stand with me in a show of solidarity in this time of crisis, I'll just have to take offense for both of us."

Aunt Iz wrapped her arms around Emilia. "Be strong, and take care of each other."

Emilia nodded and climbed into the car, shutting the door behind her.

"Take care of her, Jacob," Aunt Iz said, looking through the window at the curtain of black hair that hid Emilia's face.

"Always." Jacob hugged Aunt Iz. She felt thin to him. Breakable. "You be careful, too."

Iz smiled. "Don't worry about me."

Stone started the car, and Jacob took his seat. Iz closed the door, and before Jacob could fasten his seatbelt, the car was crunching down the driveway. Jacob looked back at the house. The last time he had left here, he had been going to New York City to stand trial. Then Emilia had been kidnapped. A war had started. Everything had changed.

"You're crowding my seat," Claire grunted from the back as she shoved Connor into Emilia.

Jacob let himself smile. That girl could sure lighten the mood.

8

ELIS

*S*tone drove for hours. They passed out of Massachusetts and into New Hampshire.

"Does the Gray Clan have territory in New Hampshire?" Jacob asked Emilia, twisting around in his seat.

"A little," Emilia said in a low voice.

Claire was sleeping, her face pressed to the car window. She had passed out after the first hour of the drive.

Connor stared out at the passing trees over Claire's head. "Clan territory doesn't follow state lines."

The car drifted back into silence as Stone steered off the main roads and into the countryside. The landscape became wilder as the hills grew taller. Stone drove across a river and farther into the trees. Sounds of the rushing water crept into the car over the *hum* of the engine.

They drove up a mountain. Jacob felt a pull in his chest. Emilia was afraid. He reached behind his seat and took her hand, trying to communicate without words, *This is a different mountain, different woods, different preserve. We won't lose anyone here. Not this place, not this time.*

The car turned onto a dirt road. Stone slowed down, driving

gently over the bumps in the road. He hadn't spoken the whole car ride. But that wasn't surprising. Larkin was his partner. He had lost someone, too. Even the strongest weren't safe anymore.

Soon there was grass growing down the center of the road. The two grooves that had been worn into the earth by tires were barely visible in the green. Trees closed in front of the car, ending the road.

Stone stopped the car, got out without saying a word, and stared into the trees.

Jacob looked back at Emilia who shrugged and climbed out of the car. Jacob followed with Claire and Connor. Together, they followed Stone's gaze into the forest. Jacob tensed as a faint rustling reached them from deep within the trees.

"What are we waiting for?" Claire whispered in his ear.

Jacob shook his head. He didn't know what they were waiting for, but whatever it was seemed to be coming at them through the woods at an alarming rate. The trees in front of them started to shake.

Claire took a step forward, peering into the shadows. Connor grabbed her by the shoulders and dragged her back to the group.

Before Jacob could thank Connor for trying to keep Claire from getting herself killed, a figure burst through the trees. It took Jacob a few seconds to process what he was seeing. Standing at least eight feet tall with the body of a horse and the torso and head of a human was a centaur.

"Welcome, children," the centaur said in a deep, resonating voice.

It was a sign of how majestic and intimidating the centaur was that Claire did not object to being called a child.

The centaur's bright blue eyes and long, curling black and grey hair reminded Jacob of a day months ago. "You're Proteus, aren't you?"

Proteus nodded. "It is good to see you again, Jacob Evans. I was not sure you would live this long."

Emilia stepped up next to Jacob, planting herself just in front of him.

"I met Proteus last year when he was skrying with Professor Eames," Jacob said, but Emilia did not relax.

"And since then, our world has broken," Proteus said.

"Isadora wanted me to thank you again for taking them in." Stone inclined his head toward Proteus. "It is a debt that will be paid."

"Send Isadora my regards," Proteus said.

Stone turned to leave.

"Thanks for the ride." Connor held out his hand.

"No problem, kid." Stone shook Connor's hand and got into the black car, leaving them alone with the centaur.

"Please meet the rest of your protectors," Proteus said, pulling their focus back to the woods and to the other centaurs peering at them from the protection of the trees.

Slowly, five other centaurs emerged from the woods.

"This is Raven." A centaur with hair so black it seemed to glint blue in the sun bowed to Jacob. "Tirsa." A female centaur nodded. Her coat was a dappled grey, and her torso was wrapped in leather sewn into a rough vest. Robin was another female with a deep red coat draped in furs so vibrantly red, Jacob was sure he had never seen an animal of that color.

Loblolly was a smaller, younger male with a rich golden coat, bright blond hair tied back in a long braid, and eyes of such pale blue, they appeared almost white. Bly, a male whose streaked hair matched the beautiful brown and white pattern of his coat, was the last to be introduced.

"It's a pleasure to meet all of you." Emilia bowed her head to the group of centaurs. The centaurs inclined their heads in return, but they all seemed to be staring at Jacob.

Raven stepped forward and gave Jacob a low bow. "We thank you for coming to our forest. You honor our Tribe by entrusting your protection and the protection of your *coniunx* to us."

"I'm sorry," Jacob said, taking a step back, "I don't think you have the right person."

"They know exactly who you are, Jacob," Proteus said. "You destroyed an evil witch who slaughtered a child of our Tribe. You gave us swift vengeance when you killed Domina."

"Jacob didn't kill anyone," Claire said. "Jacob would never—"

Proteus silenced Claire with a glance. "He killed Domina and several more of the Dragon worms."

Jacob's blood pounded in his ears. Claire and Connor didn't know. He'd never told them what had happened on the Graylock Preserve. Jacob could feel their eyes boring into him, but he couldn't bring himself to look back.

Now they knew he was a killer.

Emilia's hand slipped into his. "Jacob killed those men to save me."

"He destroyed evil to save his *coniunx*. No centaur shall judge him as cruel," Proteus said.

The centaurs behind him pawed the ground in agreement.

"*Coniunx?*" Jacob asked, struggling to hold on to the one part of the conversation that didn't involve death.

"Me, Jacob," Emilia whispered. "He means me."

Proteus strode forward and, without warning, pulled Emilia onto his back.

Emilia squealed in shock. Claire was pulled up by Loblolly and Connor by Robin.

"If you please." Bly knelt to help Jacob onto his back.

"Thank you," Jacob said, climbing onto the centaur with as much grace as he could muster.

Raven and Tirsa grabbed the four duffle bags Stone had silently left behind.

Without another word, the centaurs moved into the trees, leaving the road behind.

As they began their journey through the forest, Jacob didn't know how to properly hold onto a centaur without being rude.

With every step Bly took, Jacob rocked sideways. He glanced over at Emilia, hoping she would know the protocol for riding politely on a centaur, but her eyes were squeezed tightly shut.

Jacob wanted to go to her, hold her tight, and tell her that no fiery face would speak to them from these trees. But he couldn't promise that. He couldn't even promise they would live through the night. They were back in the woods, stuck among strangers, hoping their family would survive.

Bly's back rocked again, and Jacob's heart shot to his throat as he nearly fell sideways and onto the ground. The centaur kept walking, apparently unaware or unconcerned by the commotion on his hindquarters.

Carefully, he placed his hands on the brown and white hair that covered Bly's flanks. He squeezed his knees to keep steady and hoped he wasn't being rude. He didn't want to get them all kicked out of the only safe place Aunt Iz could find.

When Jacob's legs were so sore he was worried he wouldn't be able to stand, they came into a large, round clearing carpeted in lush grasses. Through the center ran a crystal-clear stream. Jacob took a breath and could taste the magic in the air. This place was not made by nature. The centaurs had bent it to their will.

Tents filled the clearing, standing twelve feet tall with plenty of room for even the largest centaur to stand upright. Tents of emerald green, scarlet red, bright violet, and pure white stood in groups. No two tents were identical. Some of the fabrics were plain, and others had patterns and symbols woven through them unlike any Jacob had ever seen before.

The centaurs around the clearing stopped and stared at them. Some popped their heads into tents to tell others the wizards had arrived. Some crept closer, as though hoping to get a better look. The whispers of the centaurs followed them like a breeze as Proteus led them through the clearing.

"This is where you will stay." Proteus stopped in front of an emerald green tent. Shorter than the others, it seemed to have been built for human proportions. "Rest now. Someone will come when it is time to eat." Proteus held out his hands and Emilia took them, sliding gently off his back.

Connor and Claire did the same, but Bly bowed again, letting Jacob step to the ground unassisted.

"Thank you," Jacob murmured. He wanted to say *thanks for the ride* but thought that was somehow inappropriate.

"You honor me, Jacob Gray." Bly nodded and walked away.

"Come on, Jacob," Emilia said, already halfway into the tent.

"Why did he call me Jacob Gray?" Jacob asked.

"Centaurs don't have surnames. They designate by Tribe. All of the centaurs here are of the Elis Tribe. They all use that name. You are of the Gray Clan. To them, the Gray is more important than the Evans."

Jacob's chest swelled. He liked being called a Gray. He was a part of something, even if that something was in danger. And he shared his name with Emilia.

"I can't live like this," Claire groaned, dragging Jacob's attention to the tent.

Jacob looked around. The inside of the tent was the same emerald green as the outside. A partition hung down the center, separating two sets of beds. Claire had dumped her bright pink duffle onto one of the beds where she sat pouting, clearly wanting someone to ask her what exactly was destroying her life at the moment. But Connor stood with his bag in his hand staring at Jacob. Connor raised his eyebrows, and Jacob's stomach shot up to his throat.

"Boys over here, I guess," Jacob said, leading Connor to the far side of the partition.

"Does anyone care about my needs?" Claire asked.

"Always," Emilia said.

Jacob could hear the smile in her voice.

"There is no bathroom. They gave us a tent and no bathroom," Claire said.

"Centaurs don't believe in plumbing or electricity. They live with nature. Hunt and gather. All that good stuff," Emilia said.

"So, what you're saying is they expect me to pee in the woods and not shower until the wizarding war is over?" Claire's voice rose to a carrying shriek.

"What I'm saying is be grateful we're alive and the Elis Tribe is willing to take us in."

9

THE SHADOWING

*E*milia drifted into sleep. She could feel her breath slowing as her body relaxed. Her heart beat gently in her chest. But before she could be sure she had fallen asleep, the pounding changed. It was a different rhythm. And there were other sounds, too, whispers filling the tent.

"It's ok. It's the centaurs."

"They're all following Proteus. It looks like a ceremony."

"Claire." The urgency in Jacob's voice yanked Emilia out of sleep.

Connor and Jacob stood in the tent opening, silhouetted against the night.

"What's wrong?" Emilia sat up, trying to get her mind to work.

"Oh, you know," Connor whispered, "Claire's running into the night, following a herd of centaurs beating drums. The usual."

"I'll go get her." Jacob moved silently out of the tent. Connor didn't even look back at Emilia before following.

"Always with that girl," Emilia mumbled to herself before following the boys. She reached instinctively for the sapphire pendant at her neck. She would not go into the dark without her talisman.

A long line of centaurs wound a path through the trees across the clearing, and behind them trotted Claire. Emilia ran to catch up to Jacob and Connor.

The night wind bit her bare arms, and the grass was cold and damp between her toes.

"What's happening?" Jacob whispered to her as she reached his side.

"Not a clue," she answered.

The three of them continued to run, chasing Claire's blond hair, which gleamed in the night.

Jacob caught up to Claire first and grabbed her by the arm.

"Ouch," Claire said, her voice piercing the night.

The young pale centaur Loblolly was at the end of the line, and he turned to face them. He did not speak to reprimand. *"Talahm téige."*

The ground beneath Emilia's feet became soft and warm. Loblolly turned away and continued to walk through the woods.

"What do you think you're doing?" Jacob hissed at Claire.

"Finding out what they're doing." Claire moved to follow Loblolly, but Jacob didn't let go of her arm.

"You can't go running off in the middle of the night," Jacob said.

"You never would have let me go if I'd asked. And now that they know we're following and aren't mad, why don't we keep following them before they get too far ahead?" Claire yanked her arm out of Jacob's grasp and ran down the path.

"Can't let her go alone," Connor murmured before chasing after Claire.

Jacob looked at Emilia. It took her a moment to realize he was asking her what they should do. There was no Aunt Iz here to take care of them. She and Jacob had to look after Claire and Connor now.

"Let's go."

They continued through the forest as the stars moved overhead. The ground beneath their feet stayed warm and soft as though the centaurs had rolled out a carpet for their wizard guests.

As Emilia began to wonder if they would walk all night, the drums in front of them became louder and faster, pounding like a heartbeat racing with fear.

Jacob's hand found Emilia's, and her heart began to race with the drums. She looked down at Jacob's free hand. It shone gold in the night as it swung in and out of view with every step. It looked like pure magic radiated from him.

Jacob tightened his grip on her hand as a wail pierced the night, slicing through the sound of the drums. Another voice joined the first. Then another. But Loblolly kept walking calmly onward.

Ahead, she could see the centaurs' towering shadows leaving their line and grouping around something in a clearing that was just out of sight. And still, the sound of the wailing grew louder as more centaurs added their cries.

Claire backed up, pulling Connor with her. She slipped her hand into Emilia's free one, and together, the four of them stepped into the open.

In front of them a pond sparkled in the night. The surface of the water looked like liquid diamonds that reflected a light Emilia couldn't see. Dozens of centaurs moved to surround the pond, and as each of them reached the water's edge, they raised their voices to wail. Finally, Emilia understood—they were mourning. Proteus stood across the water, tears streaming down his face as his cry rose above the others.

Emilia didn't notice the drums had stopped until she heard Proteus's low voice begin to sing. She couldn't understand his words, but slowly all of the other centaurs joined in his song. The light in the pond began to change as the water stirred, as though pushed and pulled by the voices of the singers.

Emilia could feel the magic of the song tingling her skin. A painfully sad magic. A final goodbye.

She tightened her grip on Claire's and Jacob's hands. They were there. They were with her. She wasn't alone.

A centaur with bright white hair stepped forward next to Proteus. Even across the water, Emilia could tell she was far older than any other centaur she had ever met. The centaur raised her arms, and the singing grew louder and the movement in the pond changed. The surface seemed to vibrate as the sound penetrated it, and from its center, a blackness emerged.

"Talahm siúl i scáth éineacht i lán." The song became a chant, and the blackness grew, swallowing the sparkling pond and casting them all into darkness.

"Talahm siúl i scáth éineacht i lán," the centaurs chanted faster and louder.

In the faint starlight, Emilia watched the blackness of the water overflowing the bank across from her, reaching out toward Proteus and the dozen centaurs nearest him.

She wanted to scream a warning, but the centaurs around her watched the blackness growing without fear. The darkness crept up the bodies of the thirteen centaurs until they were engulfed by blackness that blocked out even the light that had shone from the elderly centaur's hair. The thirteen became inky shadows, figures of nothing, in the night.

Air whipped around them. *"Slán a fhágáil ag duine,"* the whisper carried through the wind.

As if in answer, the chanting stopped. The thirteen centaurs made shadow turned from the pond and ran into the night. As they left the clearing, the blackness followed them, disappearing between the trees. The pond grew still as glass, reflecting the stars above, and the remaining centaurs began to leave.

"Thank you for joining us." Emilia jumped as Loblolly spoke, breaking the silence.

"What was that?" Claire asked.

"The shadowing," Loblolly said. "Our souls become shadows when we die. Tonight, some of us became shadows to run alongside the ones we love as they journey to the other side. To make sure those who were killed at Graylock make it safely to the land where shadows walk forever."

"But Proteus will come back?" Claire asked.

"They will run only until the dawn. That is as long as the spell will last."

They followed the long line of centaurs back into the woods. They walked more quickly without the regimented timing of the beating drums. Emilia jogged to keep up, Jacob keeping step by her side, and Connor running ahead. Claire panted along behind them. Emilia had forgotten for a moment how much smaller Claire was than the rest of them. Emilia slowed to walk with her, but Loblolly scooped Claire up and set her on his back.

"Thanks," Claire gasped.

"It is an honor to carry children," Loblolly said. "With them, we carry the best hope for the future."

"I wouldn't exactly call Claire anyone's best hope." Connor looped back around to Loblolly's side.

"Why did you wait?" Jacob asked, steadying Claire as she took a wild swipe at the top of Connor's head and nearly slipped off of Loblolly's back.

"Wait for what?" Loblolly asked.

"The ceremony. Graylock happened months ago. Why do the ceremony now?" Jacob said.

"We had to wait for you," Loblolly said. "The spirits of the lost ones cannot rest until their deaths are avenged. You did that. But since someone not of our Tribe avenged their deaths, their souls could not run free until our debt to you had been repaid. Bringing you here, sheltering you—this is how we have repaid our debt. Now that you are here under our protection, their souls are free."

A tug of pain pulled at the center of Emilia's chest. She glanced to Jacob. Unfamiliar lines creased his face. He looked old, filled with grief and care. She could feel something was wrong, something that hadn't troubled him a few moments ago. She tried to take his hand, but he swung it forward and out of her reach.

More quickly than Emilia would have expected, they were back in the clearing with the tents. Claire was slumped over asleep on Loblolly's back, and Jacob had to help him slide her carefully down. Jacob carried Claire to her bed. Emilia pulled back the blankets and helped him tuck Claire in.

"I swear that girl can sleep through anything," Connor muttered as he walked through the partition into the boys' half of the tent.

"Jacob." Emilia tried again to take his hand. Something was wrong. He needed her.

"Goodnight, Emilia." He disappeared behind Connor without looking back.

10

BURYING THE PAST

The tent glowed in the early morning light. Jacob lay in bed, watching as the sun peered through the fabric and made each stitch a part of a beautiful pattern, which illuminated every piece of dust that drifted by.

He didn't know how long he lay there watching the light change from grey to red to yellow. He could hear the soft thud of hooves, but it didn't make him want to get up. He wanted to hide someplace dark where no one could see him.

A bed creaked on the other side of the tent. He grabbed his clothes and dressed quickly. He was out of the tent before Emilia sat up.

Outside the tent, a small fire crackled. Food had been laid out on a table made from a roughly hewn tree. It wasn't like any breakfast Jacob had ever seen—berries, leaves, and roasted squirrel. Aside from having been skinned, the squirrel was fairly intact. The sight of the browned flesh made Jacob's stomach turn.

"Morning."

He turned to find Emilia standing behind him. Her hair was a mess. She looked warm and soft from sleep. Jacob's stomach began to purr. If he could hold her, just for a moment, hold her and keep her safe, maybe everything would be all right.

"Jacob," Emilia said.

Jacob took two long steps to the side of the tent and slapped it with his palm. "Time to get up," he called.

"Murph," Claire muttered from the other side of the fabric.

"Come on, there's food," Jacob said.

"Coming," Connor said sleepily.

"Jacob." Emilia touched his shoulder.

He turned and looked into her eyes. He knew she could feel whatever he was feeling. But he couldn't bring himself to say the words and see the understanding in her grey eyes. He didn't deserve understanding.

"Morning," Claire said, yawning as Connor dragged her out of the tent. "I thought you said there was food." She glared at the roasted squirrel.

"I bet it's pretty good," Jacob said, glad for the excuse to turn away from Emilia. He picked up the squirrel and bravely took a bite. "Not bad," he tried to speak around the stringy, dry meat in his mouth.

Claire giggled as they each took the food that scared them the least and sat on stumps around the fire. The four lapsed into silence as they ate.

Emilia took a bite of squirrel before grimacing and pushing it onto Jacob's plate. He smiled but couldn't make himself laugh with the others.

"Are you all right?" Emilia asked.

"Yeah." Jacob took a manly bite of his second squirrel.

"Is it something Loblolly said?" Claire asked, yanking Connor to sit on the ground in front of Jacob.

"I'm fine, Claire," Jacob said, trying not to choke on the strange liquid that filled his cup. It tasted like grass. He was beginning to think centaurs had a very different standard for cuisine.

Claire stared into Jacob's eyes, her childlike intuition peering into his soul. "Liar. Now fess up. What's wrong?"

"Claire," Connor said, shoving Claire's head to the side, "leave him alone."

"It's fine." Jacob pushed the food around on his plate. Somehow it felt easier to say it to someone other than Emilia. "I just…the ceremony last night. I realized I don't know where Jim, my dad, is buried. Or if he's buried. I was so busy being a wizard and trying to build a new life with all of you, I never bothered to find out."

Jacob set his plate on the ground. There was a gaping hole where his stomach had been a moment ago. But somehow he wasn't hungry anymore. He had been so caught up in trying to win Emilia, he had never bothered to give his father a proper funeral. "I'm an awful person. Jim wasn't much of a father, but that's no excuse for my being such a lousy son."

Emilia put her hand over Jacob's, and even that lightest of touches made his anger at himself begin to ease. He pulled his hand away.

"Jacob, we'll find out where Jim is," Emilia said.

"Ahem," Claire coughed. "Jacob doesn't need to worry about it. Everything's fine." Claire went back to eating her food with a guilty vengeance, gagging on the leaves she shoveled into her mouth.

"Claire," Emilia said, "what do you know?"

"Don't worry about it. Everything's been taken care of," Claire muttered, not looking up.

"What did you do?" Emilia asked in a tone that left no doubt she had been raised by Isadora Gray.

Claire glanced around at Jacob, Connor, and Emilia, her eyes dancing with an apparent desire to tell them whatever her secret was. "Promise that none of you will ever tell Aunt Iz or anyone else." Claire waited a moment. "If you don't promise, I can't tell you."

"Fine, Claire, we promise," Emilia said, though the look in her eyes was still dangerous.

"Remember a few months ago when I got in trouble for hacking and got my computer privileges revoked?" Claire paused dramatically. "Well, I hacked into the computer at the coroner's office where Jim Evans's body was and had him transferred to Fairfield, New York, and buried in the cemetery that had the highest online rating."

"Cemeteries have online ratings?" Connor's freckled forehead wrinkled.

"Everything has an online rating," Claire said quietly, staring at Jacob.

Jacob sat amazed—the void in his stomach had transformed itself into a stone in his throat. "Thanks, Claire. That was really great of you. And I can pay you back, I mean not right now, but I will."

"Oh, I didn't pay for anything," Claire said, a Cheshire cat grin spreading across her face.

"Claire!" Emilia gasped. "What did you do?"

"Easy. I took a check from Dexter's room"—Claire didn't pause when Emilia flinched at his name—"made it out to *Cash*, and mailed it to the funeral home. Why would the bank of Wayland question a few thousand dollars spent by their treasure child?" Claire looked at the shocked faces around her. "In retrospect, can anyone here really be mad at me?"

Jacob stood and pulled Claire into a hug. "Thank you, Claire. You really are amazing."

"Remind me never to let you near my money if I ever have any," Connor laughed.

"Just stay on my good side, and you'll be safe." Claire winked.

11

FROM THE EARTH

*B*efore they managed to choke down the rest of their breakfast, hooves trotted gently up behind them. The centaur Raven approached them, his black hair glinting blue in the sun.

"If you would please follow me, Grays," Raven said. "I am to take you to your lesson."

"Lesson?" Claire asked.

"Come on, Claire." Jacob lifted Claire to her feet, and they followed Raven into the trees.

"I'm just saying," Claire whispered, "if we're living in the woods with no electricity, you would think we would at least get a break from lessons."

"We have been instructed by the head of your Clan to teach you to defend yourselves," Raven said without looking back. "You should be honored. We do not allow many wizards to learn centaur magic."

"Is centaur magic different?" Jacob jogged to catch up to the centaur.

"Yes," Raven said.

Jacob paused, waiting for him to continue. When he didn't, Jacob asked, "How is it different?"

"Centaurs do not use talismans. Talismans are things wizards created. We use the magic that feeds from the earth through our hooves. We do not fight the magic, or take more than is rightfully ours," Raven said, still walking steadily down the path.

"Do you use spells?" Jacob asked. It had never occurred to him that there could be different kinds of magic. But then, he hadn't known centaurs could do magic at all.

"Centaurs do not learn magic from books," Raven answered with a hint of derision in his voice. "Our magic is passed down from generation to generation. We learn from our kind, not from lifeless pages."

"We learn from our kind, too." Claire skipped up to Raven, her head barely reaching his waist. "We just write it down in books to make sure we get it all right. Professor Eames and Aunt Iz still taught all our lessons."

Claire stopped talking when Emilia grabbed her arm.

"The centaurs have very ancient magic. And we are incredibly grateful that Proteus and the rest of your Tribe are willing to share your knowledge," Emilia said, the sweetness in her voice contrasting with the glare she shot at Claire.

"What?" Claire mouthed.

"We owe a debt to Isadora Gray for finding us new land. We owe a debt to Jacob Gray for avenging our own." Raven bowed his head at Emilia's compliment.

"I guess Iz is pretty great like that," Claire said, pulling away from Emilia to trot alongside Raven again. "And Jacob's not so bad either."

"Thanks, Claire," Jacob muttered as they reached a clearing in the trees where the grass had been worn down to hard-packed dirt. Jacob stared at the scene before him, trying to convince himself he hadn't fallen into a strange fairytale.

Archery targets lined the far side of the clearing. A child centaur with a small bow received a lesson off to one side, but the rest of the archers looked like seasoned warriors with quivers of arrows slung across their backs, calmly aiming at the targets. The high *buzz* and heavy *thud* of arrows striking their marks sounded through the clearing. Jacob spun around as a series of heavy *clangs* echoed behind him.

Another group of centaurs dueled with heavy swords and shields. Yet another group hit each other with spells Jacob didn't recognize—long ribbons of red light that lashed out like whips.

"Welcome to your lesson." Proteus strode up to them.

This was the first time Jacob had seen him since the shadowing the night before. He looked tired and worn.

"Thank you for delivering them, Raven," Proteus said.

Raven bowed and left, joining the group with the swords.

"I hope you are all well," Proteus said as he led them to the far end of the clearing.

"We're fine," Emilia said. "Thank you for your hospitality."

Jacob wanted to add his thanks but was too distracted by two centaurs charging at each other with lances. It looked like jousting, only the horse and rider were one.

"You are most welcome," Proteus said, his deep voice drawing Jacob's attention back.

"Are we going to learn to do that?" Connor pointed over to the sword practice.

"Yes." Proteus nodded.

"But why?" Claire asked. "If we're going to use weapons instead of spells, shouldn't we use a gun, or a grenade, or maybe a tank? I think a tank could be really handy."

Jacob couldn't help but agree. Swords were cool, but how much good would they do against a gun or a spell?

"Arrows and swords can be infused with magic," Proteus said without any sign he had taken offense at Claire's question. "An arrow with a spell on it can break through most wizarding shields. And a sword can be used to cut through a barrier."

"How do you know?" Claire asked.

"Wizards and centaurs have not always lived in peace," Proteus said.

Jacob didn't like the idea of fighting a centaur. Especially not Raven, who was now throttling a large, dappled centaur with his sword.

"Even now, when we live in peace with the Gray Clan, we must again fight wizards. Wizards who will stop at nothing to destroy us"—Proteus pointed at Claire—"or you."

"Actually, in this group, I'm at the bottom of the Dragons' *people to kill* list," Claire said. "It's shocking, but true."

Proteus did not seem amused.

"But still, I need to be able to defend this lot when the Dragons come," Claire added.

"Thanks, Claire." Connor patted her on the back. "I'll sleep better tonight."

"Where do we start?" Emilia asked, looking around the field.

"The first thing you must do is learn to shoot. If you wish to place a spell on the tip of an arrow, the arrow must land where you intend," Proteus said.

For a moment, Jacob thought he saw the shadow of a smile on the centaur's face.

Jacob turned, expecting to go to the targets where the centaurs practiced. But Proteus stomped a hoof, and out of the ground rose a target and four bows and quivers. The quivers were filled with arrows with shining black feathers on their shafts.

The target was larger than the ones the centaurs were using and much closer to them as well.

"We will begin simply." Proteus pulled the bow from his back.

He nocked an arrow in his bow and, without even seeming to aim, hit the target perfectly in the center.

"Sweet," Claire said with a smile. "Can I try?"

Connor crossed in front of Claire and picked one of the bows up off the ground, pulling a single arrow from a quiver. He pulled the bowstring a few times before shooting the arrow, hitting mere inches from the center of the target.

He turned to hand Claire the bow, but she didn't take it.

"What?" Connor asked, grinning at all of their shocked faces. "My parents live on a preserve. We do this sort of thing."

"Right," Claire said, nodding slowly.

It was weird to think of Connor living in the woods with wizards Jacob had never met before. But then, it was hard for Jacob to imagine other wizards who weren't trying to kill him and his family.

Proteus began teaching all of them to shoot, working with each in turn, telling them to breathe and steady the bow. By the time the sun began to set, Jacob could barely lift his arms, but he had at least hit the target. Connor had been sent to the other targets with the centaurs. Claire was showing real progress, though she kept closing her eyes before shooting. But Emilia had barely managed to get an arrow to fly, let alone hit anything.

As they made their way back to the tents, Jacob tried to walk with Emilia, but she quickened her step, hurrying in front of the rest of the group.

She was waiting at the fire outside their tent when the rest arrived. A pot hung over the flames. Jacob's stomach growled at the rich scent of the stew. He hadn't realized they hadn't eaten since breakfast. Maybe centaurs didn't believe in lunch.

"Well, that was a good day," Connor said, taking a large helping of stew and sitting on the ground by the fire.

"That's easy for you to say," Claire said. "You already knew how to do the whole *Robin Hood* bow and arrow thing. And this creepy stew probably tastes homey to you, too." Claire let some of the thick stew glop off of her spoon and into her bowl.

"Just because I know something that's useful, and you only

care about the pink computer you weren't allowed to bring out here with you, doesn't mean I like goop stew." He took a bite and shrugged. "Face it, Claire, when it comes to being out here, I'm just better at it than you."

Jacob snorted into his stew.

"It doesn't matter," Claire said with a smile. "He can be a butt if he wants. I'll have the rest of our lives to get back at him."

"Rest of our lives?" Connor raised a ginger eyebrow.

"Sure." Claire swatted him on the back of the head. "We're getting married someday, so we'll spend our whole lives together."

"Wait, what?" Emilia asked, knocking the pot of stew into the fire. Emilia started to reach into the flames after the pot but Jacob caught her hand.

"*Laevium.*" The stew pot righted itself, flying back onto the hook. The remains of their dinner smoldered on the fire.

"Sorry," Emilia said quietly to Jacob before rounding on Claire. "You're not old enough to be contemplating marriage. You're kids."

"Well, we are now." Claire shook her spoon at Emilia in a spot on imitation of Molly. "But someday, if we don't end up dying tragically, we'll grow up, and it'll be time to get married. And since Connor and I really only know each other and we'll never be able to find someone else who understands the immense trauma we've been through, we'll have to marry each other. So it only makes sense for Connor to accept right now that he's going to be my groom in a pink-themed wedding."

"I'm not wearing pink." Connor shook his head. "You do what you want, but I'm not wearing pink."

"You agree with her?" Jacob asked.

"Well, yeah, but not about the pink." Connor shrugged.

"It's all right." Claire smiled. "I have at least eight-and-a-half years to convince you."

Jacob laughed as Connor scowled silently.

Emilia stood and walked into the tent.

"Was it the stew or the pink wedding?" Claire asked as the green flap fell shut.

"Neither," Jacob said, staring at the tent.

TALAHM DELASC

*T*he green of the forest had fully changed. Everywhere she walked, Emilia was followed by the crunch of leaves. They had been with the centaurs for five weeks, and the nights had started frosting.

Emilia placed shield spells around the tent to keep in the warmth from the small fires the centaurs had given them. The blue flames—sole scorchers, Claire had taken to calling them after the third time she'd burned her foot stepping too close to the fire—licked endlessly inside iron bowls settled on the floor, but the tent was still cold at night.

Large furs had appeared on their beds a few days earlier. It took a while to get used to the idea of sleeping under an animal's skin, but at least they were warm.

Emilia rubbed her hands together, wishing they were allowed gloves on the practice field.

Jacob fought with Raven in the middle of the ring. Raven's sword shone unnaturally bright in the morning light. Emilia knew there were spells cast around the blade, but her breath still caught in her throat when Raven swung full force at Jacob's neck.

Jacob dove to the side, rolling on the ground. He caught

himself in a crouch, throwing his wand hand behind his shoulder. Out of its tip blossomed a long, red cord of light, which cracked in the air as he flung the light forward.

In one swift motion, Raven slashed his sword through the air, breaking Jacob's whip in two. The light vanished, and a grin appeared on Jacob's face as he and Raven began circling the ring.

"You must be very proud of your *coniunx*."

Emilia spun around to see the rich golden coat of Loblolly. "Uh… yes, I am." She raised her eyes to meet Loblolly's, but he was staring intently into the ring. Emilia followed his gaze, and saw that Jacob and Raven now circled the other direction.

Raven moved first, but before he could strike, Jacob raised his wand high into the air. "*Talahm delasc!*" he cried as he swung his wand downward. The red of Jacob's newly formed whip cut into the earth inches in front of Raven's hooves. Raven reared away from the spell.

"*Egrotus!*" Jacob cried. The whip shot up out of the earth behind Raven and wrapped around the blade of his sword. Jacob jerked his wand up, wrenching the sword from Raven's hand and burying it to the hilt in the ground.

Applause broke out around the ring from the centaurs gathered to watch Jacob fight.

Raven patted Jacob on the back, steam rising from his black coat in the cold. "Well done, Jacob Gray."

Claire hooted and cheered next to Emilia. Jacob ran over to them, beaming.

"Not bad," Connor said, punching Jacob on the arm. "Sorry," he added quickly when Jacob winced at the impact.

"Thanks," Jacob said, rolling his shoulder.

The crowd started to disperse, chatting merrily as they went. The centaurs were as happy as Emilia had ever seen them.

"Emilia Gray, are you ready?" Raven asked.

Emilia's heart sank. She didn't want to duel, not with Raven, not ever. She was awful at it. That's why the other centaurs had left. They were kind enough hosts to not humiliate her by watching her fail.

Jacob gripped her shoulder. "You can do this, Emi," he said quietly.

Emilia knew he was trying to be supportive, but still she wanted to scream, *No, I can't!*

"Emilia Gray," Raven said again.

Emilia tipped her chin up and strode into the ring. Her hands started to shake.

"*Talahm delasc,*" she murmured. A red whip of light, crackling with energy, appeared in her hand. "*Primurgo.*" The world shimmered for a moment as she placed the shield around herself.

Raven drew back his sword and charged her. Emilia aimed her whip for his legs, but the centaur leaped, avoiding the red light.

"Again," Raven said. He circled her, waiting for her to waver, to lose focus, to mess up.

Emilia looked at Raven's sword, which weaved like a snake, scenting the air. Its tip danced side to side, glinting in the sunlight.

Raven charged again, screaming. Emilia reacted a moment too late. Raven's blade hit her hard in the ribs, knocking her to the ground. She tried to push herself up, but the tip of the sword waited at her throat.

"Defend yourself," Raven said.

But the stream of red light had already disappeared from her hand. Her weapon was gone. She had lost, again.

"Get up." Raven lifted his sword.

Emilia lay on the cold ground. It would be so much easier to stay down, to refuse to fight.

"Come on, Emilia!" Claire cheered. "You can do it!"

Emilia looked to where Jacob and Connor stood with Claire. She could feel Jacob willing her to stand up and try again.

Emilia pushed herself back to her feet.

Hours passed. Emilia was bruised and sore from falling to the ground again and again. Connor and Claire had been taken to other lessons, and the centaurs carefully avoided her area of the clearing. She wished everyone would just come and watch her fail. It would be easier than their desperate attempts to ignore the pathetic witch who couldn't manage to maintain a spell.

"Again," Raven said.

Emilia lay on the ground, this time face first in the frozen dirt.

"No," Emilia growled.

"Again," the centaur repeated.

"There's no point," Emilia snapped. "I'll never win. I can't win."

"Then let us face each other on an equal plane." Raven sheathed his sword, walked to the edge of the hard-packed dirt, and leaned it on a nearby stump.

Emilia watched apprehensively as he slowly returned to the center of the ring.

"*Talahm delasc.*" Raven's hand glowed red as the light of his own whip sparked and crackled. "Again, Emilia Gray."

She did not want to fight Raven, but images of Samuel and Larkin floated through her thoughts.

If I had been stronger…

Emilia pushed herself up. "*Talahm delasc,*" she croaked.

Raven let out a yell as he flung his whip straight at Emilia's head. Emilia stumbled backward and almost fell out of the ring. She regained her balance and whirled her whip over her head before launching it at Raven's weapon. Raven jerked his hand out of the way just in time. The *crack* of Emilia's whip thundered around the ring.

"Yes!" Jacob shouted from behind her.

A triumphant smile had barely touched Emilia's lips before Raven's whip was in the air again.

"Talahm delascar ó cuíg!" he shouted, and the red of his whip split into five—five threads of light swirling through the air.

You see my child? Blood knows blood.

Emilia was back in the caves. Red tendrils tasted the air as they reached toward her from the Pendragon.

"No!"

A brilliant blue light blinded Emilia as she was thrown backward, her head slamming hard into the ground.

Emilia opened her eyes, blinking at the bright sunlight. She lay on the cold dirt of the practice field.

Indistinguishable shouts echoed around her. Centaurs ran to the far side of the ring where Raven lay just past the dirt in the grass, his legs sprawled limply on the ground.

"Raven," Emilia gasped, struggling to push herself to her feet. The ground seemed to twist beneath her as she stumbled toward the crowd.

"Emilia," Jacob called, running up and taking Emilia's arm to steady her. "Are you okay?"

"I'm sorry," Emilia tried to call out to Raven who was beginning to stir, but her voice came out a harsh whisper.

As Raven regained his footing, the centaurs turned to Emilia, all of their eyes trained on her pale face.

"I'm sorry," Emilia whispered again, pulling away from Jacob and running unsteadily back across the ring, away from the accusing eyes of the centaurs.

"Emilia." Jacob caught up to her and grabbed her arm, forcing her to stop. "Emi, are you okay?"

Emilia's laugh transformed into a shriek in her throat.

"Emilia Gray." A deep female voice came through the trees, followed by a rustling of leaves. A white centaur stepped into the open. She was the one Emilia had seen from across the water at the shadowing, the one who had controlled the song. Her long, white hair flowed in tangled ringlets past her waist. She wore thick furs on her torso, and her right eye was milky white. From the way she held her head to one side, Emilia was sure the old centaur couldn't see from that eye anymore.

"Sabbe." Emilia spun around as Raven spoke from behind her. He bowed to the old centaur with both hands clasped over his heart.

"Raven," Emilia said, her neck tingling as Sabbe's good eye bored into her from behind, "I'm sorry. I didn't mean to lose control."

"Emilia Gray," Sabbe repeated.

Raven bowed again and backed away, leaving Emilia and Jacob with Sabbe.

"I have come for your lesson." Sabbe tilted her head to see Jacob. "Jacob Gray, you will leave us now."

Jacob looked at Emilia. Emilia wanted to run deeper into the woods, to find a mirror and skry Aunt Iz. Beg to be brought home. But the old centaur was still staring at her.

"Go," Emilia whispered to Jacob, resisting the urge to grab his hand and make him stay with her for whatever punishment she was about to receive for losing control of her magic.

Jacob nodded and walked back through the trees, glancing over his shoulder every few feet until he was out of sight.

CHILD OF THE PENDRAGON

*W*hen Jacob was gone, the old centaur turned and made her way back into the trees. Sabbe wound through the woods, turning left and right, following a path Emilia could not see.

Emilia wanted to tell Sabbe she was sorry. That she promised to not let her magic get out of control again. But no matter how guilty Emilia felt about putting Raven in danger, she couldn't promise it wouldn't happen again. She couldn't control anything anymore, not even her magic.

Sabbe stepped into a tiny clearing, and as Emilia joined her, she raised one hand in the air. A long, thick stick appeared in Sabbe's palm. She tossed the stick into the air where it hovered five feet off the ground.

"Use the *delasc*," Sabbe said calmly, her good, silvery-blue eye staring at Emilia. "Cut one inch off the end. No running, no fighting. Focus and cut one inch off the end."

Emilia rolled her neck, trying to clear her mind. "*Talahm delasc.*" The whip appeared in her hand. She trailed the tip on the ground before throwing the whip behind her. She flicked her wrist forward and the tip of the light hit the rod, cutting off the end.

"Too much," Sabbe said. The stick grew, regaining its original length. She nodded toward the stick.

Again, Emilia tried to take just one inch off the end. The red light grazed the stick, slicing off only the tiniest portion.

Sabbe shook her shining hair, and the stick re-grew.

It took nearly an hour for Emilia to cut precisely one inch off the tip of the stick. Even in the cold she was sweating, not from movement, but from stress.

When Sabbe finally nodded, tears welled in Emilia's eyes. It was over.

"Now try." The centaur pointed at the stick, which began to sway side to side as though carried by waves.

"Fine," Emilia said, grinding her teeth. "Fine."

She stepped forward, closing the distance between herself and her now moving target. She raised her whip to strike, but before she could aim properly, the stick jolted to her left. Emilia turned her head so quickly, her neck seized. She threw a dirty glance at the centaur and felt something hard smack her between her shoulder blades.

Through tears of pain, Emilia glimpsed Sabbe's unsympathetic eye.

"Your enemies will not simply wait for your attacks."

Emilia turned away and blinked the tears from her eyes. She wouldn't let Sabbe have the satisfaction of seeing her cry. She found the stick again, floating seven feet to her right. It bobbed, mocking her by moving up and down with the rhythm of her breathing. She took a step forward, and the stick retreated a few feet. Emilia raised her whip again.

"Raven forgives you."

Emilia turned mid-strike to look at the centaur and again felt a sharp pain in her spine. The force of the blow knocked her to the ground.

"Then why are you punishing me?" Emilia glared daggers at

the aged centaur. She forced herself back to her feet, searching for her adversary. It was now directly above her, not three feet away. She poised herself to strike, but right at that moment, the stick fell out of the air, smacking her hard in the face.

Emilia wiped the blood from the corner of her mouth. She looked at the red staining the tips of her frozen fingers.

"Move faster," Sabbe said.

"No. I'm done." The whip faded from her hand.

"You cannot be done," Sabbe said. "Those who are hunted must never be done. You will never be done."

The centaur walked over to Emilia and took her hand. Not the one with the blood on it, but the one marked in gold.

"You must protect those you love. You must be strong for them. You must fight for them," the centaur said.

"I can't." Emilia yanked her hand away. "I'm sorry. I'm sorry I'm falling apart. I'm sorry I'm not strong enough to deal with this. I lost three of the most important people in my life, and I spend every second wondering if Larkin and Samuel are dead or being tortured like that bitch did to Jacob. I don't even know if I should hope they're dead, because at least then they wouldn't be in pain. And they are stuck in those caves because of me." Cracking split through the woods as branches began to rip themselves off the trees. "Because I was an idiot and didn't notice my boyfriend was a traitor who would destroy my family and my life." Emilia was screaming. The wind whipped around her, creating a tempest in the woods.

"Because of me, Jacob, Claire, and Connor got kicked out of our home and sent to these godforsaken woods so we could be trained by you to fight in a war my father started, because he's a murdering bastard. And the only person who I even want to be around is afraid to be alone with me, because he doesn't want to take advantage of a spell that tethered him to my crazy ass." Emilia stopped. Her voice echoed through the trees. Tears streamed down her cheeks. "I just can't." The branches dropped to the ground where they lay still. Emilia resisted the temptation to lie down with them.

"Instead of deciding what you cannot do, do what you can," Sabbe said so calmly that Emilia wanted to start screaming all over again. "There is a way to protect the people you love. A thing only you can learn."

"Right," Emilia spat. "Learn to fight so when Daddy dearest tries to kill us all—"

"No," Sabbe interrupted. "You think *you* must defeat the Pendragon. The only way to defeat an enemy is to understand him. Find someone who knows him. Learn what you can from that person. This is more than fighting. It is something only the child of the Pendragon can do."

"What do you mean?" Emilia swiped the tears from her cheeks. "There isn't anyone who knows the Pendragon who isn't fighting with him. Do you want me to capture a Dragon and try to make them talk?" Her stomach tightened, half-excited at the prospect of forcing a Dragon to talk.

"Can you not think of one intimate of the Pendragon who escaped?"

Emilia's stomach suddenly disappeared from her body completely. "My mother? You think my mother could help?"

"When a centaur is lost, we go back to the beginning of our trouble. You were born to live at the center of this war. That is where your trouble began. If you wish to find your path, you must go back to the beginning."

"But my mother disappeared. No one's seen her for seventeen years."

"One does not need to see something to know where it is, if you only know the right person to ask and are willing to leap without knowing where you might land." The white-haired centaur frowned, and Emilia's heart tightened. "To gain an answer, a risk must be made. To find one mother, you must risk losing the love of another. The one who knows all but feels nothing will guide you."

Emilia nodded. She didn't want to understand, but the stories she had heard as a little girl flooded back into her mind. "You really think this is what I should do? There are some places a Gray is never supposed to go. Aunt Iz will never forgive me."

"Is forgiveness more important than peace?" Sabbe asked.

Emilia shook her head.

"Leave tonight. And be well, Emilia Gray."

Sabbe disappeared through the trees before Emilia could ask why the weight of such terrible things had fallen on her.

Emilia found her way back to the training ring before slipping through the trees to the tents. No one would notice her missing. She had been gone all afternoon. All she needed was a few minutes to pack. Then she would be ready to disappear once night fell.

She walked calmly past the kitchen fires and ducked through the emerald green flap of the tent. A backpack would work best. She would need to travel light. A few changes of clothes and all of Dexter's money. Forgiveness would be a question for later. Right now, there were more important answers she needed to find.

Emilia rolled up her polar fleece and tucked it into the bottom of the bag. She tossed in clean socks and underwear. She felt Jacob behind her before he made a sound.

"I'm going." Emilia didn't stop packing. She had already made up her mind. She didn't want an argument. It would only upset Connor and Claire. And if the centaurs found out, getting away would be all the harder.

Jacob didn't say anything.

"Sabbe told me I have to go. There's something I have to do."

She turned to Jacob. He didn't try to take the clothes out of her hands or tell her she couldn't go.

"I'm going to find my mother," Emilia said quietly. "Claire figured out her name." Emilia pulled a piece of paper from her bag. She unfolded it and tried to keep her hands from shaking as she showed Jacob the printed photo of the girl with the long black curls. "Her name is Rosalie Wilde. I have to find her. Sabbe said that's where I have to start."

Emilia folded the photo back up and tucked it out of sight. She picked up her extra jeans and started rolling them, but the simple motion couldn't hide the trembling of her hands.

"Are you done?" Jacob asked, taking Emilia by the shoulders and turning her to face him.

"I can't just stay here and do nothing. I can't leave Larkin and Samuel in that place. And Iz out fighting. And if finding Rosalie could help—"

"Then we'll have to find her." Jacob sat on Emilia's bed.

Emilia shoved the jeans into her bag and dug in her drawer for a clean shirt to pack. "I'm going tonight."

"No, *we're* going tonight."

"Jacob," Emilia said, trying to keep the desperation out of her voice, "you need to stay here with Claire and Connor. You'll be safe here."

"You're not going alone," Jacob said. "And *safe* is a relative term these days."

"She's my mother. This has nothing to do with you. I don't even know if I'll be able to find her."

"You'll have a better chance if the two of us work together. And besides, there's not a chance in Hell I'm letting you go without me. And if you try"—Jacob tapped his chest right over his heart—"I can find you."

He was right. He would be able to find her. It was a part of the tethering. She could always feel where he was. Emilia tucked her shirt into the backpack. "Jacob, I know you want to come with me—"

"I *am* coming with you," Jacob corrected, taking Emilia's hand and pulling her to sit on the bed next to him.

"I'm going to the Hag." She paused, waiting for Jacob's protest, but he only slid his fingers to lock with hers. "Jacob, the Gray Clan is forbidden to communicate with the Hag. If the Council of Elders finds out, we'll be screwed."

"Emilia, there is no Council."

"If Aunt Iz finds out, she'll be furious. She'll disown me. Bind my powers. Make me a *Demadais*."

"Aunt Iz loves you. I don't think she'll disown you or banish you for talking to someone."

Emilia smiled weakly. "Yes, she will. And I don't know where the Hag is. And if I find her, she might not even agree to speak to us, and if she does, she might not tell us anything. And if she does, we still might not be able to find Rosalie. And if we do find Rosalie, it might not do us any good."

"Sounds like you're against going." Jacob took Emilia's chin and turned her face to his.

"I have to. I need to know—" Emilia couldn't finish the sentence. She didn't know what questions she needed answered, only that the questions existed and that this was the place to begin.

"Then we're going together. And that's final. I'll pack my bag, and we'll leave tonight." Jacob pressed his forehead to Emilia's.

Emilia closed her eyes and allowed herself a moment to relax. One quick breath in peace. Jacob smelled like the forest after a rain. "Claire and Connor..." She willed herself back to the moment.

"They'll be as safe here without us as with. Safer, actually." Jacob stood and crossed through the curtain to the boys' side of the tent.

~

*E*milia lay in bed, her heart pounding. She could hear the guards pacing the perimeter of the camp, but the fires had stopped crackling. Everyone who would sleep tonight was already in bed. Emilia pushed her covers slowly aside. She had gone to bed with her clothes on. Her sneakers were unlaced and waiting for her next to her backpack under the bed. She slid them slowly out and pulled on her shoes. Claire sighed, and Emilia froze, her heart beating in her throat. Minutes passed, and Claire's breathing slowed, becoming even.

Emilia stood and quietly slipped her pack onto her back. She looked at Claire, her blond hair splayed out on her pink pillow, contentedly sleeping, safe and warm. Tears welled in her eyes. Claire would be so hurt. Emilia was abandoning her. She bent down and gently kissed her head.

"I'm sorry," she whispered before slipping out of the tent into the cool night air.

"You ready?" Jacob whispered from the shadow next to the tent.

Emilia spun to face him.

Jacob smiled. "Do you think I didn't know you'd try to sneak off without me?"

Emilia smiled back. "I'm glad it didn't work."

1 4

RUNAWAYS

*T*hey snuck quietly through the camp. Centaur guards paced the outside of the settlement every night, making sure no Dragons could hunt them while they slept.

Emilia led Jacob to the farthest corner of the camp.

Jacob's heart raced, his pulse thundering in his ears. How good was a centaur's hearing? Would they be able to hear his heart's desperate attempts to leap out of his chest?

Speckled white and brown hide shone in the moonlight. Jacob pinned Emilia behind a tree as Bly swung around, looking for the source of the faint rustling they had made as they moved through the forest. Jacob held his breath, waiting for Bly to keep moving. A branch snapped much closer than Bly had been only moments before.

"*Invectus,*" Emilia murmured. A warm breeze whispered past Jacob's skin, and the air around them shimmered. A moment later, Bly appeared next to them, looking directly at them, but Jacob knew he could only see the tree.

Bly's breath felt hot on Jacob's neck, but he turned and stalked away through the trees.

"Nice one," Jacob whispered into Emilia's ear.

"I know," she answered with a smile before leading him deeper into the woods.

The night breeze whispered around them. But they met no one else.

"Shouldn't there be more guards?" Jacob searched through the shadows for some sign of life.

"You would think."

But still they saw no one.

Up ahead, a stream glistened in the moonlight, six feet wide and flowing more slowly than Jacob had ever seen a stream move.

Jacob pulled out his wand and pointed it at his feet. "*Calaridus.*"

Emilia looked at him, one eyebrow raised.

"I hate having wet socks." Jacob shrugged.

Jacob stood at the edge of the water. Even in the quiet woods, he could barely hear the murmur of the stream. He stepped into the water and felt nothing. His feet had remained dry.

"I'm brilliant," he said quietly to Emilia, before noticing that something was wrong. Horribly wrong.

His feet had been on solid creek bed only a moment before, but now he was sinking, and fast. As he tried to pull his foot up, the water around him began to shake.

"Emilia, don't step in," Jacob said, but Emilia was already staring in horror at the opposite bank. Jacob followed her gaze and knew in an instant what scared her. The other side of the water had gotten father away. Jacob struggled more, and as he did, the water again grew wider.

"Jacob, stop moving," Emilia said, her quiet voice filled with panic.

"I would love to, Emi, but I'm sinking!" Jacob was up to his waist now. As though he had been wearing waterproof boots, the water now flowed freely around his feet, stinging them like ice.

"Just hold still," Emilia said.

"Great, I'll be right here."

Emilia turned to the tree behind her. The light from her sapphire pendant glowed blue on the tree's bark. *"Colubra me bratus."*

One of the branches of the tree began to snake itself down toward Emilia as she continued to chant. She gathered the branch in her hand like a rope.

"Terminora," she finished. "Catch the end."

She threw the end of the branch-turned-rope to Jacob. A bit of it touched the water, and looking behind him, Jacob watched the water grow wider yet again.

"Hold on tight," Emilia said.

Jacob wrapped the rope around his wrist, expecting Emilia to try and pull him out of the water, which he wasn't sure she could do. Emilia may be a talented witch, but he was bigger.

"Evedeo," Emilia said, and in one swift and squelchy instant, Jacob was soaring into the air. The rope whipped itself from his grasp as it turned back into a normal branch, and Jacob tumbled to the ground, landing in a heap at Emilia's feet.

"You all right?" Emilia asked as she reached down to help Jacob up.

Jacob gasped as pain seared through his arm at her touch. "I think I dislocated my shoulder."

"Sorry." Emilia grimaced. "But on the bright side, you're not sinking anymore."

"Yeah, thanks for that," Jacob said through his teeth as he stood, feeling the rest of his body smart with the bruises forming from his fall.

"Exhale," Emilia said.

"What?"

"Paricio."

Jacob stifled a shouted curse as his shoulder popped painfully back into place.

"Thanks," Jacob grunted, turning back to look at the stream. It was twenty feet wide now and running fast. "Now we know why there aren't more guards. They drown intruders instead."

He scanned up and down the stream. It ran through the trees and out of sight. "I don't think we can go around."

"No need. *Denursus.*" The branch turned back into a rope and landed at Emilia's feet.

"You couldn't have pulled me out gently then?" Jacob asked.

"I needed more power. I may have overestimated, but still, no drowning." Emilia handed the rope to Jacob.

"I think the water's too wide to swing across." Jacob shook his head, handing the rope back.

"A rope swing ruined my life once. I learned how to make these things do exactly what I want." Emilia settled herself into Jacob's arms, and his heart began to race. "Ready?"

Jacob held tight to the rope.

"*Volitus!*" Emilia cried.

Before Jacob could ask what he was supposed to be doing, they were flying over the water.

It was impossibly wide. As they passed over the creek, it seemed to grow wider still. The speed of their swing raced with the expansion of the water. The rope was nowhere near long enough for them to land on the other side. Jacob pulled Emilia closer to him, preparing himself for the fall into the cold water, but they kept swinging out over the far bank.

"*Crestundo!*" Emilia cried. The rope cracked like a whip, sending them toward the ground. Jacob twisted in mid-air, and Emilia landed on top of him with a squeal.

"Oops." Emilia pushed herself up enough to look Jacob in the eyes. "I guess I've never tried that with two people before."

She was so close to him. Jacob could feel her heart pounding on top of his. The hum in his chest grew stronger as her faint scent of lilac reached him.

"Jacob," Emilia whispered.

Her face was only inches from his. All he had to do was raise his head from the ground, and their lips would meet.

"Jacob." She leaned in closer to him.

Jacob stood, knocking Emilia to the ground. His heart tried to beat out of his chest. "Great, I'm glad we made it across."

Emilia didn't say anything. He felt her confusion wriggling through his mind. He shook himself and turned back toward the water. It was now wider than any river he had ever seen and rushed past at a furious speed. Squinting, he could barely make out the bank where they had been only a minute before.

"No going back." Emilia stood beside him.

"No going back."

OUT OF THE WOODS

"*B*orluxeo," Emilia murmured. A tiny light appeared in front of her. The light spun around itself, creating a glowing sphere.

Jacob covered his ears as the light let out a high, ear-piercing whistle before shooting directly at his head. Jacob threw himself onto the ground, rolling over in time to watch the light shoot off into the woods to his right.

Emilia started walking left.

"What was that?" Jacob stared after the light.

"That was north," Emilia called back to him. "We want south." She didn't look at him as they continued through the woods.

They trekked for miles through the dark forest. As the sun broke through the trees, Jacob wondered if the centaurs knew they were gone yet. Would the expanding stream have alerted them that someone had gotten out of the camp? Would they be searching for them right now? Or would Claire wander around camp calling for them, Connor trying to calm her tears when they realized Jacob and Emilia were gone?

"We should have left a note," Jacob said.

"And said what?" Emilia glanced back at him. *"We're leaving, but we can't tell you where we're going or when we're going to be back. Mostly because we don't know either of those things?"*

"That would have worked. Connor would have appreciated the humor. Where *are* we going, anyway?"

"First, we find a road. Then we find a ride," Emilia said, finally stopping. She gazed out into the forest.

It was beautiful. The sun lit the changing leaves and filled the woods with a golden glow.

"I don't know what we do after that," Emilia said, continuing her march through the trees.

Another hour later, Emilia burst through a bramble of branches and whooped. "I found it!"

Jacob caught up and saw a road. A wonderful, two-lane road.

"Nicely done," he said, smiling at Emilia.

"Thanks." Emilia beamed back. "Now, we need a ride."

He looked up and down the road, but there were no cars in sight.

"Or we keep walking till we find a ride." Emilia sighed and started down the road.

A rumble sounded behind them, and Jacob turned. A blue truck was driving up the road. Jacob took a step back as Emilia waved her arms at the car. But the truck sped by.

"Really?" Emilia shouted after the truck.

"It's all right." Jacob took her arm, pulling her out of the middle of the road. "We can keep walking."

"Fine," Emilia said.

A car came whizzing down the road in front of them.

"*Auravecto,*" Emilia said. The car's front passenger side tire popped. The car swerved wildly before pulling over with a sad *thunk, thunk, thunk.*

"Emilia," Jacob growled as a middle-aged woman got out of the car and stared at her front tire.

The woman cursed loudly.

"You all right?" Emilia called to the woman. "That was a bad piece of luck."

The woman looked behind her, noticing Jacob and Emilia for the first time.

"Yep." The woman shook her head and walked around to the trunk.

Emilia shot Jacob a prompting look. "Ask if she wants help."

"You want some help?" Jacob asked, walking toward the woman. He had no idea how to change a tire. He knew it involved nuts and a jack, but he had never owned a car.

The woman looked Jacob up and down. "Sure. I don't actually know how to do this."

"Good thing we were here," Emilia said as she reached into the trunk. She took the woman's wrist and muttered, "*Immemoris.*"

The woman's eyes unfocused.

"Emi," Jacob hissed.

"Just put her in the back seat," Emilia said, slamming the trunk shut.

Jacob grunted as he lifted the deceptively heavy woman into the car.

"*Aureddo.*" Emilia's voice came from the front of the car, which leveled out as the tire reinflated. Emilia dusted her hands off as she climbed into the driver's seat. Jacob ran around to the passenger's side. The woman giggled feebly in the back.

"Are we actually stealing a car right now?" Jacob asked as Emilia turned the car around and sped down the road.

"We are *borrowing* a car," Emilia said, her voice crisp. "Just until we get to the next town with a bus station and a computer. I mean, we are trying to stop an evil killer here."

"All right." Jacob leaned back in his seat.

"I steal a car and wipe a woman's memory, and all I get is an *all right?*" Emilia rolled her eyes.

"Yes." Jacob smiled.

Emilia sped more quickly through the woods than Stone had. And she didn't seem to mind which side of the center line she drove on.

"Do you want me to take over?" Jacob said, keeping his voice light through his clenched teeth as Emilia veered back into the right lane when a car raced toward them, blaring its horn.

"Oh, relax," Emilia said. "We'll be fine."

They were traveling a different road than the one Stone had used when he brought them to the preserve. After a few minutes of driving through the tall trees of the old forest, they reached houses that surrounded a lake.

It took less than twenty minutes to find a town. Emilia drove around for a while, looking for a bus stop.

"You know, driving is harder than you'd think," Emilia said after nearly hitting a car while trying to make a left turn.

"That's why humans have lessons for this sort of thing," Jacob said, trying to keep himself from grasping the handle at the top of the door.

Emilia pulled up outside a coffee shop advertising free internet.

"You can relax," she said as she turned off the engine. "We're here."

Jacob climbed out of the car and looked up and down the street. People went about their morning business on their way to work without pausing to stare at the two teenagers who had *borrowed* a car.

"What do we do about her?" Jacob asked, gesturing to the woman now snoring loudly in the back seat of her own car.

"She'll be fine in an hour or so."

Jacob chuckled as Emilia counted out enough coins to cover the hour on the parking meter.

"We don't want her to get a ticket for giving us a ride." Emilia shrugged, then turned and walked into the coffee shop.

"*Giving us a ride* seems like a bit of an understatement," Jacob whispered. "Please tell me you're not going to mess with someone's memory so we can borrow a computer."

"No." She shook her head, and her black hair flew around her. She looked like she could laugh. Like she was actually happy. But then, this was the first time they'd had something real to do in months. They weren't locked in a house waiting for bad news or standing in a ring, playing with magical whips. They were doing something.

Emilia walked up to a young man who was working on his laptop. "Sorry to bother you, but I lost my phone, and I need to check something online." She pulled a fifty-dollar bill from her pocket. "Can I borrow your computer for ten minutes?"

The man passed over his computer without a word. Emilia handed the man the fifty and Jacob a twenty. "Will you grab breakfast?" she asked. "To go," she added before sitting down to stare at the computer screen.

Jacob stood in line, glancing back at Emilia every few seconds. She typed while the man she had borrowed the computer from sat next to her, keeping watch over his possession. Jacob ordered two muffins and two coffees and paid the overly cheerful cashier.

"Have a great morning," she told Jacob with a smile that showed nearly all of her teeth.

He made his way back to Emilia, cradling the coffees and the muffin bag. Jacob had never bought breakfast before. He had never bought anything at a coffee shop or restaurant before. He had never had the money.

"Thank you," Emilia said to the man as she passed the computer back at the same time Jacob arrived.

The man nodded.

"And do you know which way the bus station is?" Emilia asked.

The man pointed.

"Thanks," Jacob said as Emilia steered him out of the shop.

"Did you find the Hag already?" Jacob whispered.

"No," Emilia said, "but I found someone who knows where to find her."

"Who?" Jacob asked, stepping onto the sidewalk and heading in the direction the man had pointed.

"Do you remember me telling you that Mr. Proctor was almost kicked off the Council of Elders because of his nephew?" Emilia sipped her coffee.

Jacob thought back to the Council meeting in New York. Jacob had been accused of being a rebel, of helping the Dragons in their attacks. The Council had barely released him when he and Emilia heard the beginnings of the wizarding war they were all now a part of. That was the night Emilia had been captured. But through the haze of remembered fear, he could almost see Emilia sitting on a shiny desk, telling him something about a nephew getting Mr. Proctor into trouble.

"Maybe," Jacob said after a few moments.

"The nephew went to talk to the Hag. The Council found out and made him a *Demadais*," Emilia said, and then she laughed, the bright sound echoing through the sleepy street.

"Is binding his powers funny?" Jacob asked. He pointed at a blue sign with a bus on it, and they turned onto another street.

"No, but making your new last name *Demadais* is. I can't imagine the Council liked that. But it works for us," Emilia said, putting a hand up in front of Jacob. He had been so distracted by what she was saying he had almost walked into traffic.

"I thought we were going to have to find his last address under his old name and go from there, but I know exactly where to find him. All we have to do is get ourselves to Carlisle, Pennsylvania, and we've got him." Emilia stopped outside the bus station.

Already, people were piling on and off buses.

"You're brilliant," Jacob said.

"Thank you," she said softly, giving him brief but genuine smile. She took his hand and steered him to the ticket counter.

"I'd like two tickets to Carlisle, Pennsylvania, please."

The man behind the ticket counter stared at them for a moment before shrugging and turning to his computer. "Round trip or one way?" he asked.

"One way," Emilia answered.

"I can get you on a bus outta here in a half hour. With layovers, you won't get into Carlisle till tonight. Or you could be good kids and head back to school." The man eyed Jacob.

"Thank you for the advice, sir," Jacob said as politely as he could manage, "but we'll take the tickets."

"Ninety-eight dollars then," the man said, holding out his hand.

Emilia reached into her bag and pulled out a crisp hundred-dollar bill.

The man took his time, holding the bill up to the light, making sure it was real before opening his cash drawer and handing them their tickets.

"Thank you," Emilia said as she took them.

The man said nothing in return as he passed them two crum-pled dollar bills.

"What was his problem?" Emilia asked as they searched for seats inside the station, ready to wait for the first of three buses they would be riding that day.

"He thought we were running away together," Jacob said quietly, hoping the bus would come soon. Would the man call the police for two runaway minors?

"We *are* running away together. We just aren't running from school. Well, at least not like he's thinking. And we're going to do something important. And it's none of his business, anyway." Emilia glared at the man at the ticket counter before turning back to look out the window.

She was right. They had run away together. He had snuck off

with the girl he loved in the middle of the night. The sneaking off part was easy. The love part was much harder. And keeping them both alive? Jacob sipped his coffee. They would figure that out as they went.

LILACS

he bus rides were long and boring. Jacob stared out the window, but Emilia kept scanning their fellow passengers.

"What are you looking for?" Jacob finally asked halfway through the second bus ride.

Emilia glanced around for a moment before whispering, "Last time we used mass transit, the Dragons tried to have us killed."

"The Dragons don't know where we are." Jacob studied the crowd on the bus.

Emilia followed his gaze, but still she couldn't find anyone with a dragon tattoo wrapping from their cheek to their neck— the mark the Dragon warriors wore.

"How could they know we're on this bus?" Jacob asked after a moment.

"Theoretically, they couldn't," Emilia murmured.

"Good." Jacob sat back in his seat. "Besides, I don't think the man from the airplane is in any state to come after us. Between you melting plastic in his ears, and me using him to get through the Dragons' shield, I would be surprised if Laurent is even alive."

"Laurent?" Emilia asked, feeling Jacob tense in the seat next to her.

"In the woods," Jacob said, looking back out the window. "He was with two other men. One of them called him Laurent."

"You think the Pendragon killed him?" Emilia whispered.

"Domina, the woman from the caves."

The woman who tortured him. Emilia slipped her hand into Jacob's, holding on tightly.

"She said he was going to be punished. Since you got out…"

Emilia looked around, but the passengers close to them didn't appear to have noticed their talk of the Dragons. It seemed strange to speak of a magical war on a bus surrounded by humans.

"There's no way the Pendragon would let him live," Emilia whispered. "If you hadn't gotten in, I wouldn't have gotten out." Emilia leaned against his shoulder. Jacob sighed. Emilia closed her eyes. She was exhausted. They were runaways, but in that moment, everything felt right.

When the bus finally arrived in Carlisle, it was nearly midnight. People sleeping on benches or curled up on the floor lay scattered around the station. They didn't look homeless, just stuck. Stranded in a florescent-lit limbo.

"We should take turns keeping watch," Jacob said, his gaze following a man who crept through the sleepers.

He didn't touch anyone, but the way the man stared at every woman he passed made Emilia's skin crawl.

"Or we could find a hotel." Emilia pulled Jacob to the ticket counter where a woman sat reading a magazine and chewing gum.

"Hi," Emilia said.

The woman looked up with a glare that implied Emilia had interrupted something truly important.

"Do you know where we could find a hotel?" Emilia asked.

The woman pointed across the street. Out the window a motel sign flickered feebly in the darkness.

"Only place nearby." The woman grinned, smacked her gum, and turned back to her magazine.

"Great, thanks for your help." Jacob dragged Emilia away and through the glass door.

Emilia looked up and down the street. Cars honked in the distance, their noise joining the shouts of the bar hoppers making their way through the night.

"Are you sure we should be staying here?" Jacob asked, stepping closer to Emilia. Having him close, his arm brushing against hers, made her feel safe. Even if there were sirens coming closer.

"We'll be fine," Emilia said, pulling away from Jacob and starting across the street.

"Hey, honey," a voice called from down the street. A group of men lurched toward them, stumbling out of a bar. "Why don't you come spend the night with a real man?"

"How about you back off," Jacob shouted, rounding on the men.

Emilia felt Jacob's anger rise in her own chest. She grabbed his arm and dragged him to the other side of the street.

"Don't worry, baby. I'll find you later," the drunk called after her.

"Leave it," Emilia said as she pushed the motel door open.

"If they knew what—"

"What we are? What you could do to them?" Emilia asked, trying not to smile. "Yes, I'm sure they would leave me alone. But we don't need the attention of a street fight right now."

"No fighting allowed here," an old man grumbled from behind the desk. "We don't want any more blood in our motel rooms."

As she went to the desk, Emilia tried to keep herself from wondering why there had been *any* blood in the rooms, how much there had been, and how good a job they had done cleaning it up.

"Don't worry," Emilia said, giving her most winning smile, "there were just some people cat calling."

The old man didn't seem convinced.

"We'd like a room for the night," Emilia said, still smiling.

"I'll need some ID." The man fished a pair of glasses from his pocket. "We don't take under eighteen without a parent. And you pay for the whole night."

"Sure." Emilia slid her backpack off and set it on the floor, kneeling next to it.

Jacob crouched beside her and mouthed, "IDs?"

Emilia shook her head and pulled out her wallet. Tucked in behind the cash were two IDs—hers and one Dexter had left behind. Her stomach dropped as she looked at the picture. "*Inmutatio nomino.*" Dexter's dark hair was replaced by Jacob's blond. The skin darkened, and the picture became Jacob.

"*Inmutatio numerus.*" The dates on Emilia and Dexter's IDs faded, and when the black ink blossomed back onto the cards, they were both twenty years old.

"Here you go." Emilia stood and handed the IDs to the desk man. "And we'll be paying cash for the room."

The man grumbled to himself as he handed Emilia forms to sign, glaring at Jacob all the while.

Finally, he passed Emilia the electronic key. "Keep it clean," he growled as they left the dingy lobby.

They climbed up the cracked cement slab staircase to a room on the second floor. As Emilia opened the door that had *221* written in black marker, the scent of cheap cleaner and stale smoke hit her in the face.

"It's fine," she said, trying to look like she hadn't made a horrible mistake by bringing him here. "I can fix this."

She went into the room, and Jacob followed, turning on the lights. The bulbs blinked for a moment before flickering on. The room was small and suffocating with one bed in the center.

Everything in the room was a greyish-brown color, clearly chosen to hide filth.

"Wait," Emilia said as Jacob went to set his bag on the ground. "*Pestiola.*" All of the surfaces in the room began to glow. "*Ablutere.*" Instantly, the carpet was lighter and the bureau shined. "*Malundo.*" A strange buzzing came from the direction of the bed as the sheets seemed to shift of their own accord. "*Bellusavis.*" With a sharp pop, the glow faded, and the room looked like a perfectly normal yet much cleaner version of itself.

Emilia took a deep breath. Fresh lilac. "That's a bit better." She turned to Jacob. He stared at her.

"So that's how you do it." Jacob's brow wrinkled.

"Do what? Clean the room? Molly taught me cleaning spells forever ago." Emilia tossed her bag onto the bed.

"That's why you always smell like lilacs." Jacob sat in the lone chair behind the door.

"I smell like lilacs?"

"Always," Jacob answered, not looking at her.

Emilia's cheeks flushed. Of course he would know her scent. He knew her better than anyone else.

Emilia started pulling things out of her bag. Toothbrush, clothes.

"How did you get his ID?" Jacob asked.

"It was in his room."

"Sure," Jacob said after a long moment.

Emilia could hear the hurt in his voice. Did he think she missed Dexter?

"When I smashed his room"—Emilia sat on the bed—"I found a bag. It had some cash and his ID. I don't know why he had it. Maybe it was just Dexter being a jerk and keeping lots of money around because he could. Maybe he was going to run. I don't know. But there was no point in leaving a few thousand dollars behind."

"A few thousand?" Jacob asked, his eyes wide.

"In a leather satchel in his closet." Emilia nodded. "I was going to burn it, but I didn't want to look at it. Then when Iz sent us to the Green Mountain Preserve, and it was going to be the four of us on our own, it seemed stupid not to have a backup plan. So I packed it all." Emilia looked at Jacob, willing him to understand she had kept the ID not for Dexter's photo, but as a way out. A way out she and Jacob now needed.

"It was a good plan." Jacob reached out and took Emilia's hand. She felt the hum in her chest begin.

"I thought so, too." She looked into Jacob's eyes. So blue and so tired. "We should get some rest." It seemed like days since she had lain in her bed in the tent across from Claire.

Jacob looked at Emilia and then at the bed. "I'll take the chair." He reached down to untie his shoes.

"Jacob, don't be silly," Emilia said, even as her cheeks flushed. "It's a big bed, and we can share. Neither of us slept last night."

"I'll be fine in the chair," Jacob said, taking more time than a person needed to untie his shoes.

"I'll feel too guilty to sleep if you do that." Emilia stood up, toothbrush in hand. At least the sink looked decent after her spell. "I promise I'll even let you have some of the covers."

By the time they were both ready for bed, Emilia could hardly breathe. Why was she panicking?

It's only Jacob, she told herself. But the other, much softer voice in her mind answered, *But he is the rest of your life. He is your comfort. He is your match.*

When Jacob turned off the light, she moved as close to the edge of the bed as she could, digging her nails around the edge of the mattress. As she drifted into sleep, Emilia wondered what it would be like to sleep on the other side of the bed, where she could find comfort in his arms.

17

DEMADAIS

*T*he sun breaking through the thin curtain woke Jacob the next morning. He could hear voices outside. The bus station must be busy. He turned onto his back and felt Emilia lying next to him, warm and soft. She was sleeping peacefully. No nightmares last night. Her black hair spread out over the pillows like a cloud of silk. Jacob watched her breathing slowly. He hadn't seen her look this calm in months. He checked the clock. Only 7 a.m. If he slipped out to buy her breakfast, she could sleep longer.

Carefully shifting the sheets, he climbed out of bed and dressed, quietly taking some cash from Emilia's wallet before slipping out of the room. The morning was bright and cool. Jacob looked up and down the street. There had to be food somewhere nearby. He spotted a little place next to the bus station. It had a neon sign that read *Coffee* and another that flashed the word *Open*.

Jacob made his way over, cutting through the crowd of grumbling people milling outside the bus station who had spent their night on buses coming from somewhere. When he entered the little café, Jacob immediately wished he had listened more carefully to Emilia's cleaning spells.

"What you want, honey?" a harassed looking woman asked when it was his turn at the counter.

Jacob looked in the glass case. "Two bagels with cream cheese and two coffees."

The woman shuffled down the glass case, preparing his order. "Eight bucks." The woman held a hand over Jacob's bag.

Jacob handed the woman a twenty and picked up the bag and two coffees. Fear stabbed through him. Panic and worry.

Jacob turned and bolted through the door.

"Honey, your change!" the woman called after him.

Jacob raced across the road. A car horn blared at him, but he didn't stop to look. As he approached the door marked 221, it flung open before he could reach for the handle.

"Emilia!" he shouted.

Emilia whipped around, her black hair flying behind her as she launched herself at Jacob.

The coffee hit the ground as Jacob pushed Emilia aside ready to fight whoever had been attacking her in the room. But the room was empty.

"What happened?" Jacob asked, taking Emilia's arms and searching her over for signs of damage.

"I woke up and you weren't here," Emilia said, staring at the spilled coffee. "I thought you'd left." Her voice faded as she bent down and picked up the now empty coffee cups and the surprisingly dry paper bag.

"Emi," Jacob whispered as she avoided his eyes, "I'm not going anywhere. Wherever we have to go to figure this thing out, we're going together."

"I know that, I do." Emilia pulled the food from the bag. Jacob watched the bagels shake in her hand. "I just—"

Jacob wrapped his arms around her. He wanted to say something wonderfully brave like, *I fought Domina to save to you.* Or something romantic like, *You're half of my soul, Emilia. I could no sooner leave you than rip my heart in two.*

But when he felt Emilia relax in his arms and her heartbeat slow, he knew he didn't need to say anything. She knew it all already.

They ate in silence before packing their backpacks and heading to the motel lobby. There was a different, younger man at the desk. It took Emilia a few minutes to convince him that she really did want a cab, even if it was going to be more than forty dollars to get all the way across town.

When she wasn't looking, the man gave Jacob a nod and a thumbs up. Jacob blushed, half in anger, half in embarrassment. Luckily, the cab arrived soon, and they climbed in, leaving the motel and the hungover people on the street behind. The cab sped them out of the grungy outskirts, past the town center, and into the suburbs.

The neighborhood could have been in Fairfield. It was strangely normal. There were children running through piles of leaves and men on ladders, cleaning house gutters in preparation for winter.

Jacob watched through the window of the cab as women pushed strollers down the streets in packs. How could a *Demadais* live here? Were wizards brainwashed when their powers were bound?

The driver stopped in front of a white house with red shutters. The lawn was perfectly manicured and surrounded by a white picket fence.

"You're sure this is the right place?" Jacob murmured.

"How many Marshal Demadaies' do you think there are in the world? This has to be him," Emilia whispered as she handed the driver cash for the ride. "If you wait for us, I'll pay the fare and tip you an extra twenty."

"In cash?" the driver asked, peering at them in his rearview mirror.

"Cash," Emilia said with a smile as she slid out of the car. "Ready?" Emilia asked as Jacob closed the cab door.

"Sure. But you never actually met this guy?" Jacob asked. "I mean, do we just walk up to the door and say, *Hi, we know you were banished, but we're wizards and we'd really like to meet the person who got you all outcast and stuff?*"

"First of all, you are a wizard, I am a witch. Second, calling the Hag a person is a stretch. And third, I have a plan, so let me do the talking." She sounded confident, but Jacob could feel her nerves bouncing.

He opened the perfectly oiled gate. "After you."

Emilia walked past him and up the sidewalk. She didn't pause before pressing the doorbell.

The bell rang, but Jacob didn't see any signs of life. Emilia kept pushing the bell over and over.

"Emi, maybe we should just go." There was a *creak* on the stairs, and a shadow moved toward them in the house.

Emilia smiled at Jacob as the door opened.

Standing in front of them was a man wearing a t-shirt and jeans and looking as thoroughly unlike Mr. Proctor as anyone could imagine.

"Can I help you?" the man asked. He looked normal and happy.

Surely, Jacob thought, *this man hasn't been banished.*

"Hi," Emilia said, "my name is Leah and this is James. We were sent here by your Uncle Proctor."

The man's face turned a horrible greenish-grey. "I think you must have the wrong house," he said quickly as he tried to push the door closed.

Jacob stuck his foot in the doorway, stopping the man from shutting them out of the house.

"Actually, I don't think we do," Emilia said. "But if you would prefer, we can come inside and discuss our business quietly rather than on your porch."

As if on cue, a woman called from behind them, "Marshal, the kids loved your wife's brownies at the bake sale. Do you think she would give me the recipe?"

"Sure," Marshal said with a smile. "I'll have her bring it over to you." He waved as the woman thanked him and continued down the street. "Get inside," he whispered.

The inside of the house was as normal as the outside. Jacob hadn't realized how accustomed he had become to the chaos of living in a magical house. Aunt Iz kept normal human appliances and conveniences at the Mansion House, but there was always something *more* there. Something indescribably wonderful. A life and an energy that Jacob associated with magic.

The man led them away from the big windows that surrounded the front of the house and into a small living room in the back. There was a large comfy couch, an armchair, a rocker, and an infant's play mat on the floor.

"What do you want?" Marshal asked, not offering Jacob or Emilia a seat.

"One simple question. How do we find the Hag?" Emilia asked without missing a beat.

"Are you serious?" Marshal spat. "I spend thirteen years as an outcast, and now two kids show up at my home asking about that." Marshal paced angrily. "Is the Council trying to check on me? Make sure that I've been a good boy? Well, you can tell my uncle to go straight to Hell. The Council ruined my life once. I won't let them do it again. I have a wife and kids. I'm an accountant, for God's sake. I've done nothing wrong. You have no right to be here."

"We weren't sent by the Council," Emilia said. "In fact, there isn't a Council these days."

"I knew it." Marshal lowered himself onto the couch "All of the things that have been happening, horrible things no one can explain. I knew it was magic."

"You're right." The color drained from Emilia's face. "Horrible things are happening. The Magical Community is at war. And I need you to tell me where the Hag is."

"If you aren't from the Council, I don't have to tell you anything." Marshal stood up and pointed to the door. "I don't want any magic in this house. If wizards are fighting, I want nothing to do with it."

"If you wanted nothing to do with magic, you should have picked a different last name. *Demadais*? It wasn't even hard to find you." Emilia planted her feet.

Jacob looked back and forth between the two of them standing across from each other, glaring.

"I made a foolish choice when I was young," Marshal said through gritted teeth.

"Choosing that name, or seeing the Hag?"

"Both. But I have accepted my punishment. I will not let my family suffer—"

"No one needs to suffer. Just tell us where she is, and we'll leave," Jacob said.

Marshal looked at him, seemingly surprised that Jacob could speak.

"I haven't seen the Hag in thirteen years," Marshal said softly. "I don't know if she's still there."

"Where?" Jacob asked.

"Bellevue Avenue in Newport, Rhode Island. The Hag lives in a mansion that looks out onto the ocean. You'll know it when you get near it. You can feel the magic. At least I could before."

"Thank you," Emilia said, moving toward the door.

"Thanks." Jacob followed her.

They were back out in the crisp air when Marshal called after them. "Wait." He ran down the steps and stood close to them, looking around nervously. "If the Council is gone, you could unbind me. I could have my magic back."

"Mr. Demadais, you have a family," Jacob said.

"They wouldn't need to know," Marshal said desperately. "I could use my magic to help my family. To protect them."

"I don't know how to undo a binding," Emilia said. "We can't help you."

"There has to be a book with the spell. You can go. You can find it," Marshal pleaded, grabbing Emilia's hand in both of his.

"I don't know where we could find it. I don't know where a book like that would be." Emilia tugged her hand away from Marshal. "The Council controlled those spells."

"Maybe we can ask the Hag?" Jacob said, placing himself between Emilia and Marshal.

Marshal leaped back. "Don't ask her. Don't mention me to her." The man backed toward the house, stumbling when his heel hit the porch stairs. "Don't you ever come back here again." He ran up the steps and slammed the door. The lock clicked loudly behind him.

Jacob took Emilia's hand and pulled her through the white picket gate, away from the house and back into the cab.

"He seemed to like your visit," the cab driver said as they slid back into their seats.

"Family friend," Emilia said, still looking at the house. "Could you take us to the bus station please?"

"Can do." The driver pulled away from the curb and the perfect houses.

"So what do we do now?" Jacob whispered in Emilia's ear.

"Get a bus ticket to Newport and find the Hag," Emilia said.

"Why was Marshal so terrified of the Hag?" Jacob asked. "I can understand being afraid of what the Council would do if they found out you did something forbidden, but it seemed like he was afraid of her. Who is the Hag?"

Emilia glanced at the driver in the rearview mirror. "There are some kinds of magic that have been lost. Spells even the Council didn't have records of. The Hag used one of those spells on herself. I don't know what it did to her, but she's powerful.

And she knows things that normal people couldn't." Emilia chewed on her bottom lip.

Jacob watched out the window as they passed back into the filthy part of town. What would be waiting for them in Newport?

"I'll take that cash," the cab driver said as he stopped in front of the bus station.

Emilia paid the driver. "And your tip." She handed him an extra twenty.

Jacob followed her as she wound her way up to the ticket counter. "Two tickets to Newport, Rhode Island, please."

Just like normal people, Jacob thought as he and Emilia carried their backpacks onto the next bus out of Carlisle.

Were their fellow passengers traveling for work or play? Were they going on an adventure to a new place or to visit family? Were they trying to find a mythical person to save family?

Emilia began to laugh. It started in her throat as a tiny giggle, but soon she was laughing so hard her face turned red, and the people near them on the bus were staring at her.

Jacob leaned against the window, smiling.

He didn't laugh along or even ask what was funny. He waited while tears ran down Emilia's cheeks.

She gasped a few times and finally stopped, choking a little as she tried to breathe normally.

"Better?" Jacob asked, still smiling.

"A bit, yeah," Emilia giggled. "This is completely absurd, isn't it?"

"Absolutely absurd." Jacob nodded.

"And we're going to do it anyway?" Emilia asked.

"Yep." Jacob leaned back in his seat, looking out the window as the bus pulled out of the station.

"Okay then." Emilia lifted Jacob's arm, inserting herself next to his side.

His heart leaped as she placed her head on his shoulder.

"I've never been to Rhode Island before," Emilia said, watching the slums pass slowly by.

"I've never been anywhere before," Jacob said.

She laced her fingers through his. Like he was the only thing she had left to hang on to.

Jacob kissed her forehead. Emilia closed her eyes. They were together. Together, they could survive anything.

18

THE MANSIONS OF BELLEVUE

The bus pulled onto the long bridge that would lead them to Aquidneck Island. The leaves shone orange and gold in the bright sunlight. Jacob looked down at Emilia sleeping peacefully on his shoulder. He wanted to keep watching her sleep, but he couldn't let her miss this view.

"Emi," he whispered, rubbing her arm. "Wake up."

Jacob pointed out the window, and Emilia's sleepy eyes followed. The water glistened, and Emilia smiled.

"It's beautiful," she said. "Are we there?"

"Soon," Jacob said.

The other passengers were beginning to gather their things.

"Good." Emilia nodded. "I want to get this over with." She ran a hand through her hair, pushing it away from her face, before starting to chew on her bottom lip.

"Don't be nervous," Jacob said, trying not to smile. She only ever chewed her lip when she was nervous. "The Hag will see us. We'll make her."

"That's what I'm worried about." Emilia leaned in to whisper to him. "My whole life, all I've heard is how dangerous she is.

And now we're going to walk up to her house and ask for a favor. If anyone finds out…"

Jacob wrapped his arm around her. "No one will ever know."

"But if they do—"

"They won't." Jacob brushed back the veil of black hair that hid Emilia's face.

"But if they do, they'll bind our powers. Jacob, they'll make us human."

"Don't worry," Jacob said, looking back out the window as the bus pulled into town, "I lived as a human for most of my life. It's not that bad. I'll show you how it's done."

Emilia smacked his chest and chuckled. "You won't leave me alone?" she said, her voice soft but serious. "I don't think I could live like that alone. Promise me."

Jacob pulled her closer. "I promise. Whatever happens, we're in this together."

Emilia laid her head on his shoulder as the bus pulled into the station.

This place was as different as possible from Carlisle. The bus station was clean and bright, right near the shining water. Shops and restaurants lined the wharf, and a line of cabs sat outside the station.

"Shall we?" Jacob gestured to the cabs. Emilia nodded, and they climbed into the nearest yellow car.

"Where to?" the driver asked cheerfully.

"We'd like to go to the mansion on Bellevue," Jacob said.

"You need to be a little more specific," the driver said. "Bellevue is full of mansions."

"Right," Emilia said. "Can you take us to where the mansions start, then?"

"Can do," the driver said. "But if you don't know which one you're looking for, you better be ready to do a whole lot of walking."

The town was packed full of tourists. It took more time for

the driver to wind through the crowds than to drive the short distance to Bellevue Avenue.

"Here you go." The man stopped in front of a huge house made of stone.

Sweeping steps led out of the mansion and onto the mani-cured lawn. Sculpted hedges grew throughout the grounds. Everything was perfectly placed.

Emilia paid the man, and he handed her a card in return. "Call if you get tired of walking."

"Thanks." Emilia pushed the card into her pocket.

"Now what?" Jacob asked, gazing down the tree-lined street.

People bustled past them in groups being led from one house to another, touring the great mansions. The street stretched in front of them and twisted out of view. There could be hundreds of houses on Bellevue, assuming Marshal had even told them the right street.

"Should we go door to door?" Jacob pictured them walking up to each of the elaborate front doors, knocking, and asking if a magical Hag lived there.

"We start walking and hope the Hag has enough magic for us to be able to notice." Emilia slipped her arm through Jacob's and led him down the street. To anyone else they would have looked like two teenagers on a date, not two wizards trying to find a Hag.

When Jacob had moved to the Mansion House, he thought that was as big as houses came. He was wrong. Even though the Mansion House had more space than he could ever imagine using, it was small compared to these homes. If you could even call something the size of a palace a home.

Walking past each of the mansions was surreal, like some-thing out of a fairy tale that didn't belong in a world with cars and tourists. The houses had massive grounds to match their grandeur, with gardens full of flowers and fountains. On one side of the street, the houses backed right up to the ocean.

Emilia pulled Jacob across the street to walk closer to those estates.

"Do you feel something?" Jacob asked as Emilia paused in front of one of the smaller mansions. A grand weeping willow covered the front of the house, its tendrils swaying in the breeze.

"No." Emilia shook her head. "It's just that Aunt Iz would love that tree."

Jacob wrapped his arm around Emilia's waist. "We don't have to do this. We could find another way. Get Claire a computer and see what she can come up with."

"She already tried." Emilia sighed and continued down the street.

They walked for miles. Emilia would pause in front of some mansions and walk straight past the ones with hordes of tourists piling out.

A crowd cut in front of them, intent on getting into a mansion with a wide, sweeping lawn. But Jacob didn't notice what all the tourists were cooing about. A few houses down, a tall iron gate cut through a high brick wall. Gold shone in the center of the gate.

"Emilia," Jacob whispered, trying to make out what the gold could be. He took Emilia's hand and started dragging her down the street.

"What?" Emilia looked behind them into the throng of people. "Is someone following us?" she asked as Jacob sped up to a run.

He stopped in front of the gate and pointed at the gold that glinted in the light. They were symbols. Clan symbols. A crow sat above a sword that was engraved with a wand. A crescent moon was surrounded by three stars. A falcon with its wings spread wide was mixed in with eight other symbols, some that Jacob didn't even understand. And in the center of them all was a tree— the tree of life that was the crest of the Gray Clan.

"I think I found it," Jacob said, his skin prickling with the horrible feeling of being watched by an unseen person. "I think the Hag is here."

Emilia nodded. She raised her hand to place it on the gate, but before she could touch it, the tree of life and the crescent moon with three stars began to glow. The gate hummed for a moment before swinging silently open.

Emilia laced her fingers through Jacob's. He saw the fear in her eyes, but together they stepped through the gates.

As soon as they entered the grounds, Jacob knew they were in a place flooded with magic. He could smell it. Even though winter was coming, the grass was still a bright emerald green. The changing leaves on the trees shimmered like someone had sprinkled diamond dust on each one. The air was infused with a tang of salt that filled Jacob's lungs, and the moment he took a breath, he no longer felt tired or hungry. Just alive.

"She's here," Emilia said. "She has to be here."

Jacob studied the mansion in front of them. White marble housed delicately latticed windows. A huge front door of intricately carved wood was the only entrance in sight.

Together, they walked up to the door. The closer they got, the more details of the carvings Jacob could see, and the stranger they became. The carvings seemed to be of scenes that were all somehow connected.

In the top left panel, a beautiful woman looked out on the ocean. Below, the same woman was surrounded by men. She rose above them as they reached toward her in adoration. In the bottom left panel, a man held the woman lovingly in his arms, and the other men stood below them, their backs turned toward the woman in anger.

The top right panel showed the men surrounding the woman, holding pitchforks and clubs. The man who had been holding her now lay at her feet, dead. In the next panel, the woman soared above a pyre, ropes falling from her body, and the men around her writhed on the ground, suffering. In the last carving on the bottom right, the woman ran into a great forest as all the people left alive turned away from her.

The longer Jacob stared at the door, the more the images appeared to move. Only slightly, but enough to make them seem alive. Jacob knelt to look more closely at the woman in the last scene. Her face looked stricken, but there were no tears on her cheeks as she ran.

Without a sound, the wooden door swung open.

"Ready?" Jacob stood.

"Ready," Emilia said, and they walked into the house.

19

THE HAG

A faint breeze tickled the back of Jacob's neck. He turned to see the door shutting silently behind them.

They stood in a huge hallway. A ballroom opened in front of them with windows looking out onto the ocean. The hall was lined with large doors on either side, but there was not a single person in sight.

Emilia pointed toward the ballroom. It was the only open door and the only source of light.

Jacob nodded, and they started forward, the thick carpet muffling their footsteps so the silence remained. They reached the foot of a staircase that ended next to the ballroom doors. As they passed the stairs, the doors to the ballroom slammed shut with a *boom* that echoed through the house. Jacob pulled Emilia back, searching for someone who could have closed the doors, but they were still alone.

Jacob's blood pounded in his ears like a muffled drum as the silence returned. Emilia led him back toward the other doors. The rumble of a sliding door to their left pulled Jacob's gaze toward a room with light blue walls adorned in white, but as he took a step forward, the doors snapped back together with a loud *bang* that seemed to shake the air around them.

Crashes from the other end of the hall were coming closer, creeping steadily toward them as more and more doors added themselves to the din.

Crash, crash, crash.

Jacob clapped his hands over Emilia's ears just as all of the doors in the hall opened and slammed at once with a sound like a cannon that ripped through the house.

Jacob swallowed hard as the ringing in his ears sent the room swaying.

"Up we go?" Jacob asked, lowering his hands from Emilia's ears.

"I think that's what she wants."

Jacob followed Emilia up the ruby red-carpeted stairs. The staircase turned back on itself before reaching the second floor. Jacob expected to see another hallway, with more slamming doors. But in front of them was a silk curtain of deep violet.

"Welcome Emilia, daughter of the Gray Clan," said a voice from behind the curtain. The voice didn't sound centuries old. On the contrary, it sounded light and musical. "I did not think I would ever meet another member of my Clan. Although, I suppose you are not truly a Gray."

Jacob took Emilia's hand.

"And Jacob Evans. The boy with no family and one of the most powerful enemies in the world."

Jacob's spine tingled at the use of his name. How much did the Hag know about them?

A hand slid through the curtain. A pale, smooth hand with nails painted bright red. The violet curtain was carelessly tossed aside, and a gorgeous woman sauntered through. She was small, not much more than five feet tall, but her nude satin pumps added at least four inches. A white silk dress clung to her hour-glass curves, and her dark brown hair hung in seductive waves around her shoulders. Her painted red lips slipped into a smile as she laughed. "And I was afraid this decade would be boring."

The woman waited patiently for either of them to speak.

Emilia managed to find her voice first. "I'm sorry, we were sent here to find the Hag of the Gray Clan. Do you know where she is?"

The woman tossed her head back and laughed again. "I am the Hag, you silly child."

"But you're—" Jacob began.

"Beautiful, gorgeous, forever young?" The Hag walked to Jacob and ran her cold fingers gently across his cheek, lingering on the circular scar that Domina had given him. "If children were told the truth about Hags, there would be far too many of us running around. And then I wouldn't be special anymore." She pulled Jacob's face so close to hers they were nearly kissing. "Come, my beautiful boy, and we shall see what the future holds for you."

The Hag laced her fingers through Jacob's and began to pull him through the curtain. Emilia started to follow.

"Did I say you were invited?" the Hag asked without looking back.

"No," Emilia said, "but Jacob's not going anywhere with you unless I go, too."

"Fine." The Hag tossed her hair and glared at Emilia, her red lips pouting. "But sometimes three does become a crowd."

The light on the other side of the curtain was dim, without any of the cheer that filled the bright afternoon. Fine silk pillows and cushions lay scattered carelessly across the floor. There was a table in the center of the room, and upon it sat a crystal ball, a small bowl that emanated violently green smoke, and platters of food. Chocolates, berries, and pomegranate seeds on a silver tray lay next to drinks in crystal decanters.

"Please eat," the Hag said as she laid herself on a sofa of pillows. "I do love watching people eat. I haven't tasted anything in, oh, a few hundred years or so."

Jacob looked to Emilia.

"We're not hungry, but thank you for the kind offer," she said as she pulled Jacob to sit next to her on a pile of pillows near the curtain, keeping them close to an exit.

"Dear Izzy taught you well." The Hag clapped her hands, and all the food disappeared. "Pity. There was nothing wrong with the food. The two of you are far too interesting for me to enchant. You will provide much more entertainment for me out in the world than if you were to stay here with me. Although," she smiled seductively at Jacob, "it will be a pity to let *you* go."

Emilia cleared her throat.

"I know," the Hag said, tossing her hands dramatically into the air, "he's taken, like it or not, forever and ever. But a girl can still dream. You have dreams, don't you Emilia? Dark dreams that wake you up with fear and tears."

Emilia stiffened.

"What's your name?" Jacob said, trying to steer the conversation away from Emilia's nightmares.

"I am the Hag of the Gray Clan."

"But—"

"I have no other name. I did once, a long time ago. But when you choose to live forever, certain sacrifices must be made. One is the luxury of a name. I cannot eat or sleep. I cannot feel cold or heat. I cannot feel the sun or the wind or the rain on my face. I feel nothing." The Hag ran her fingers along her silken pillows. "They could be as rough as stone, and I would never know. But it is a small price to pay."

"It seems like a lot to give up." Jacob squeezed Emilia's hand. What would it be like to never feel the warmth of her skin again?

"Not for me," the Hag said, quickly standing up and moving to the far wall of the room. She pulled aside another violet curtain to reveal a window that overlooked the ocean. The sun was beginning to set, and the sky was filled with colors. The Hag's eyes reflected the red of the setting sun and became frighteningly fierce.

"When I was a witch, the humans believed in magic. They hunted us. They burned us. They would praise God as they roasted us alive. And not only witches. They burned humans, too. Just because their neighbors had accused them of witchcraft. They tried to burn me once. I escaped. And that's when I decided being immortal was worth being shunned. It was worth every sacrifice to be beyond the power of simple humans."

The Hag strode to Emilia, her eyes still blazing, and took Emilia's chin, examining her face. "It is forbidden by the laws of your Clan for you to speak to me. And yet you come here. Tell me why, Emilia Gray. Why would you betray Isadora?"

"Because I need your help," Emilia said softly, holding the Hag's penetrating gaze. "I need information. There was a woman. I'm told she came to you seventeen years ago. I've tried to track her, and this is as far as I can get." Emilia paused, but the Hag said nothing. "I need to find this woman. It's very important."

"Coward." The Hag tossed Emilia's face aside and strode back to her couch. "If you can't even ask the question, why should I give an answer?"

"But that is my question. I want to know where she is." Emilia rubbed her neck.

"Ask the question you came here for, Emilia Gray, or leave me be."

Emilia took a deep breath. "I want to know where my mother is. I want to know why she came to you, what she asked you, and what you told her."

The Hag smiled and closed her eyes. "Why do you want to know where your mother is?"

"Because she's the only person I know who lived in the compound where LeFay is based and managed to leave it alive."

"You were in the Graylock caves for days. Even I didn't know if you would make it out alive. And it is rare for me not to know how a story ends." The Hag sat up, her gaze drinking in Emilia and Jacob. It was as though she were trying to absorb their essence. "I cannot see how either of your stories end. And your tales are carefully linked with the fate of all Magickind. I haven't felt this interested in anything in three hundred years. It's almost like being alive again."

"You're not alive?" Jacob asked, unable to pull his eyes from hers.

"One cannot be considered truly alive if one can never die. There is more of stone than of tree in me, Jacob Evans."

"I was a prisoner," Emilia said, startling Jacob, who wrenched his gaze from the Hag's, "I never got to explore anything. I don't know how LeFay works. My mother could be an excellent resource."

"That isn't why you want to find your mother. I may not be able to see your future, traitor of the Grays, but I know your heart. You want redemption. You want to know that your mother was a good little witch. That half of your blood is not stained with death. That the Pendragon has good in him somewhere." The Hag laughed. It was a high, cold cackle unlike her earlier mirth.

For the first time, Jacob was afraid. He could feel the Hag's age and power seeping into the room. The Hag stopped laughing. Her face became cold and her voice low.

"What if I tell you that no good awaits you down this path? You will find neither the answers you want nor the peace you seek. Would you leave this house? Go back to your home and pretend you had never met the outcast of your Clan?"

"No," Emilia said, her face calm though her voice shook. "I would find another way."

"When the first flash of dawn breaks through the night
at the top of the land where the rock meets the sea,
the first to see and the first to take flight
will find the land of Her pure delight.

The chance of the fall is the price must be paid.

Risk darkness or light to find what awaits.

"That is what I told Rosalie, and that is all I will tell you."

Jacob began to ask the Hag what the poem meant, but Emilia squeezed his hand, tears streamed down her face.

"And you, my beautiful boy," the Hag said, resuming her coy smile. "What question would you ask?"

Jacob's stomach clenched. He hadn't come with a request. His only thought had been of helping Emilia. His mind raced. There were many things he wanted to know. The Hag began drumming her fingers on the couch. A steady rhythm. *One-two-three-four, one-two-three-four.*

"I want to know—" Jacob stared down at his hands. His left palm glowed gold. "How did I survive? When we were escaping the Dragons. I did a spell. I had no talisman, and I lived. Why?"

"Why are you alive?" The Hag leaned toward him, her eyes unblinking. "Is it such an awful thing to be mortal these days? I thought you would enjoy all of the earthly pleasures." Her eyes flitted to Emilia, and the Hag smiled. "But if you've grown tired of being a fragile little mortal, I could make you like me. We could live in my palace forever. The spell has been lost, banished from all the books, but I remember how to become like me. After all, I did it to myself." The Hag reached toward Jacob. "We would have such fun."

"No," Emilia said. "He will not be joining you." Jacob looked at Emilia, the tears had disappeared from her eyes, but her face had turned red. "We thank you for your extraordinarily kind offer."

The Hag shrugged and leaned back in her seat.

"But, do you know how I survived?" Jacob dared to ask again.

"Sometimes, the universe hasn't finished with you." The Hag shook her head disinterestedly. "All things are linked, and the bind makes us strong. Perhaps you will find out why. Perhaps it was all just a mistake."

"But aren't you supposed to know these things? Can't you just tell me?" Jacob asked. "Ma'am," he added lamely.

The Hag smiled and stood, her hips swaying as she walked away to the far end of the curtain.

"Then can I ask you another question?" Jacob said, his heart leaping. "How can we defeat the Dragons?"

The Hag shook her head, but this time she did not smile.

"But you have to know how the Dragons can be defeated. You can see the future," Jacob said desperately.

"I can sense the future, silly child. I don't watch it like a pantomime."

"Is there a weakness we can use?" Jacob asked. Again, the Hag shook her head. "Is there a spell we can use to defeat them?"

"Darling, I do magic. What you're asking for is a miracle." The Hag pushed through the curtain and was gone.

20

LITERAL TRANSLATION

*E*milia took Jacob's hand and led him back through the curtain. Resisting the urge to run down the stairs, she walked calmly, her eyes fixed on the front door. She kept waiting for the doors to slam again, or for darkness to stop them. But before she could reach the front door, it opened without a sound, and the pale blue of twilight poured into the house.

Emilia pulled Jacob through the door and quickened her pace. They walked silently across the lush, green lawn. At the gate, the tree and the crescent moon with three stars glowed gold for a moment before it swung open, and Emilia ran the last few steps back out onto the sidewalk. Without a word, she turned and started walking back down Bellevue Avenue.

Emilia didn't look back at Jacob. She just kept walking, dragging him along. Her neck tingled as though the Hag were still watching her, wanting to see what would come next. They walked in silence past the rows of mansions, their windows lit up in the dark night. They all looked welcoming. A place with a bed and a shower. A place to hide in safety.

"What do we do now?" Jacob finally asked when they were nearly back to town. "We could try to contact Claire. See if she has anymore leads on who else might know what happened to your mother."

"Don't bother," Emilia muttered and started walking faster.

"I know this is frustrating, Emi, but you can't give up." Jacob took Emilia's shoulder. "Just because the Hag didn't want to tell us anything helpful, about anything at all, doesn't mean we should give up. We'll find another way."

"I'm not giving up." Emilia turned to Jacob. "But you're going back to the preserve."

"What?"

"We'll buy you a bus ticket," Emilia said, trying to push through what she had to say.

"No!" Jacob shouted before looking around and pulling Emilia to the edge of the sidewalk. The people passing them were staring now. They probably wondered if Emilia was in danger. They were right. "If I'm going back to the preserve, so are you."

"But—"

"No buts. Where you go, I go." Jacob held Emilia's gaze.

"You can't come with me. Not where I'm going." She tipped her chin up, trying to look confident.

"What do you mean?"

"The Hag told me exactly what she told my mother."

"You mean that poem? It was just a bunch of nonsense." Jacob shook his head. "The Hag was just screwing with us. Probably the most fun she's had since cars were invented."

"It's an old legend. At least, I thought it was a legend, but if that's what the Hag told my mother, it must be real." Emilia yanked her hands through her hair. She turned and continued walking. "And I need to go, because if that's where she is," her voice caught in her throat, "then I have to rescue her."

"You think the poem is about something real?" Jacob asked, his voice rising above a whisper for a moment.

"The Hag doesn't lie." Emilia took Jacob's hands. She could

feel his fear for her radiating through her chest. "And I can't let you come with me. Jacob, I can't put you in that kind of danger."

"We just went to a forbidden Hag," Jacob said.

Emilia dropped his hands and covered her face. He didn't understand.

"There are Dragons out there hunting us every day. I won't let you go alone." Jacob lifted Emilia's hands from her face. "We're in this together, remember?"

"That was before I knew where I was going," Emilia whispered.

"What does the poem mean?" Jacob asked, wrinkles forming in the middle of his forehead.

"I thought it was a fairytale," Emilia said. "A legend about a faraway place where everything is peaceful and perfect."

"What place?"

"The Siren's Realm. A place travelers go where they're safe forever." Emilia began to tremble.

"If it's a safe place, then why would your mother need to be rescued?" Jacob asked.

"The Siren doesn't exist in this world. She exists on a plane slightly out of sync with ours. At least, that's what I've always been told. But I thought it was a story. I never really considered the possibility that the Siren might be real. The legend says the Siren's world is stitched to ours with thread spun of time and magic. Everywhere one of those stitches exists, there's a way to slip from our world into hers, through the hole the thread makes.

"Lots of wizards and witches have tried to cross into the Siren's Realm, but none of them come back. Iz always said it was because the Siren wasn't real, and they died trying to get to her. But if some of them made it..."

"So, how do we start looking?" Jacob asked without hesitation.

Emilia sighed. She wanted to protect him, to make sure at least he was safe. But he would be able to find her, and what if she couldn't do it alone? "My mother was last seen in Maine, so I say we start there."

Emilia found them a room in a nice hotel with windows overlooking the water. She used a memory charm on the concierge who insisted he needed a credit card number for security purposes. She ordered room service, ate quickly, and ran down to use the computers in the lobby. She didn't speak to Jacob, and he hadn't said a word either. But he followed her, letting her use magic on the concierge without protest, eating the food that came, and following her downstairs without question.

Emilia stared at the computer screen, wondering where to start. Before she could begin typing, Jacob put his hand over the keyboard.

"Just a minute," he said. Emilia looked at him, wondering what argument he had been forming in his silence. "Is it safe to search this on the internet?"

"What?" Emilia asked.

Jacob looked behind him, making sure they couldn't be overheard. "I started thinking about it in the coffee shop where you borrowed that guy's computer. The MAGI computer system, Spellnet, it tracked everything, right?"

Emilia nodded.

"Including the ability to track search terms?" Jacob asked.

"I'm sure it could have, but I never thought to ask." Emilia reached for the keyboard.

"Then maybe you shouldn't search something like this. What if the Dragons have access to the system? They could find us here." Jacob lifted Emilia's hands away from the keys.

"Claire crashed the system. There is no more Spellnet. No MAGI. And I don't know how else to figure out what the poem means. If you have a better idea, I would love to hear it," Emilia said.

"When MAGI was broken into—" Jacob began.

Emilia shivered. MAGI had always been tough, unbreakable, until it was gone.

"—Iz thought there could have been someone on the inside. Maybe whoever the spy was is still out there with access to some of the Spellnet things. They could—"

"Could what?" Emilia asked. "There is no way to do this safely."

Jacob held Emilia's wrists for another moment before letting go.

"Thank you," she said, trying to decide what to search first.

Jacob pulled his chair to the computer next to her and began typing. Emilia looked over at him, one eyebrow raised.

"If we're going to do this, we should at least make it quick," Jacob said as he began typing.

After two hours, Emilia's eyes began to blur. Other hotel guests kept peeking in, hoping to use one of the computers, glaring when they realized she and Jacob were still using the only two.

They tried searching disappearances in Maine, where Rosalie had last been seen. They looked for places rumored to have a connection to the Siren, but there was nothing at all about her. They looked for any mystical rumors, but other than a few scattered ghost stories, there was nothing.

Emilia dug the heels of her hands into her eyes. They were going about this all wrong. There had to be a way to find the information.

"Emi," Jacob whispered, "recite it to me one more time."

"When the first flash of dawn breaks through the night
at the top of the land where the rock meets the sea,
the first to see and the first to take flight
will find the land of her pure delight.
The chance of the fall is the price must be paid.
Risk darkness or light to find what awaits."

"I think I might have it." A smile spread across Jacob's face.

Emilia stood and leaned over his shoulder, expecting to see a page about the Siren, but instead he was on a national park site.

"Cadillac Mountain is the first place in America to see the sunlight each morning. People climb to the top to be the first to watch the sun rise from the peak of a giant rock, next to the ocean," Jacob said.

"So the poem is literal?" Emilia asked, scanning down the information on the page.

"Yep," Jacob said, "and the kicker? It's in Maine."

Emilia kept reading the page. It sounded right. The rock near the water, the first flash of dawn. It all fit. "That means the jumping is literal, too."

Jacob nodded. "Sounds like it."

"We're going to go to Maine, climb a mountain, and then jump off of it?" Emilia asked, trying to keep her voice from shaking.

"And hope we land in a magical place of joy and light, find your mom, and save the day. I think that's the plan," Jacob said calmly. He reached up and slid his hand into Emilia's. She held on as tightly as she could. "We'll be fine."

"Jacob," Emilia said, sitting back down and pulling her chair close to his, "you don't have to do this. You don't have to jump off a cliff for me."

Jacob let go of Emilia's hand and started typing again, pulling up bus schedules.

"Jacob," Emilia whispered.

"Do you think jumping off a cliff with you would be worse than staying on solid ground and watching you do it alone?" Jacob asked, not looking at Emilia.

The room went blurry again as tears formed in Emilia's eyes. "We should take a train." She rolled her chair back to her computer. "You've never been on a train, right?"

"Never," Jacob said.

"We should fix that," Emilia said, looking at Jacob and trying to make herself smile.

When Emilia had folded up the printed train schedule and tucked it into her pocket, Jacob took her hand and led her through the hotel atrium to the shining glass elevator.

"It's not too late," Emilia said, pressing the button for the fifth floor. "I say we drop off our backpacks and go find some food."

"Are restaurants open this late?" Jacob asked as the elevator began its smooth ascent, gliding past the hotel rooms and the balconies overlooking the fountain and elegant tables that decorated the open atrium.

Emilia smiled. There were so many things she took for granted that Jacob had never done. "Have you ever had clam chowder?" Jacob opened his mouth to speak, but Emilia placed a finger over his lips. "It doesn't count if it's from a can."

Emilia tumbled into Jacob and knocked him hard into the back wall as the elevator gave a sudden and violent jerk. Emilia scrambled to her feet, rubbing the center of her forehead where it had smacked into the glass wall.

The lights in the elevator flickered feebly, and shouts carried through the glass from the lobby four-and-a-half stories below. Emilia looked down out of the glass window. People in hotel uniforms ran around the lobby.

"It's okay. They know we're stuck," Emilia said.

Jacob was already at the elevator door, pushing the emergency button. "Should we try and pry the doors open?"

The elevator gave another grinding lurch and dropped a foot. Jacob grabbed Emilia, pulling her to his chest.

"Yes," Emilia said, her heart beginning to race. "I think opening the doors would be a yes."

21

CORNERED

*J*acob crammed his fingers into the crack, straining to pull the doors apart.

"Jacob, back up." Emilia placed her hands on the doors. "*Portalaxio.*"

With an earsplitting shriek of metal, the doors opened a few inches.

"Well, it's a start."

The horrible noise vibrating from below their feet began only a second before the elevator slammed into the wall to which it was braced.

Emilia stumbled and grabbed the handrail that circled the glass for support.

Screams of terror carried up from the lobby.

"Emilia, I don't think elevators are supposed to do that," Jacob said, pulling Emilia to the ground.

Emilia crawled toward the glass, trying to see below.

"Emi." Jacob grabbed her hand to pull her back.

"If someone is attacking us, I would like to know who." Emilia scanned the chaos on the ground floor.

Mothers dragged their children from the lobby. A police

officer waved people away from the base of the elevator. The hotel manager shouted into a walkie-talkie he gripped close to his mouth. But there was no one focusing on the elevator. No one marked with a dragon tattoo.

"I don't see who could be doing this," Emilia said.

The elevator shook violently, and with a wail worse than nails clawing a chalkboard, it rose a few feet.

"This is definitely magic, right?" Jacob crawled back to the doors and wedged his fingers into the inches-wide crack Emilia had made.

"Yes." Emilia twisted to look at the people lining the balconies on each of the floors. Dozens of people stared at the elevator, and the crowd grew larger by the second.

"Could this be the Hag?" Jacob asked.

There was a sharp *pop*, and a crack appeared in the glass of the elevator.

Emilia squinted past the growing crack, and there, standing across the atrium on the fourth floor balcony, was a man. His head was covered by the hood of his coat, but Emilia could see the gleam of victory in his eyes. He was a hunter who had cornered his prey, waiting for the right moment to make the kill.

"Jacob, I can see the one doing the spell," Emilia said quickly, lying against the floor as she slid her pack onto her back. "I'm going to crash the elevator to the ground floor. You blow the doors out, then we both run like hell for the street."

"People will see." Jacob tightened the straps of his pack.

"Ready?" Emilia said. These humans were already seeing magic. They didn't need to see her and Jacob die, too. "One, two, three! *Deoressum!*" Emilia shouted, and for one brief second, the elevator fell in silence, before the crowd began to scream.

Jacob's cry of *"Magneverto,"* and the resounding *boom* of the doors exploding joined the din.

Emilia screamed, *"Pulvaura,"* and the elevator gave one giant bounce as though stopped by an air bag.

Jacob seized Emilia's hand and dragged her through the elevator doors and out into the hallway.

The people on the ground floor ran from the explosion Jacob had created to free them from the elevator. Emilia held tightly onto Jacob's hand and pulled him into the mass of humans surging toward the front door of the hotel.

After a few seconds of being bumped and knocked by the others fleeing, they were out on the street and into the wonderfully cold night. Emilia gulped in the crisp air as she tried to steer Jacob through the now stationary crowd.

Most of the guests stopped just outside the hotel. Whether curious to see what would happen next or unwilling to abandon their belongings, Emilia didn't know. They broke through the crowd and onto a street that ran along the wharfs.

"What do we do?" Jacob kept pace with Emilia as she fought the urge to run.

They needed to blend in. Find someplace out of the way to think or hide. The water was lined with restaurants all shining their bright lights into the night. They couldn't go in there. She wouldn't risk the lives of humans by trying to hide in a crowded place.

Up ahead, a patch of darkness cut between the lines of shops and restaurants. This wharf wasn't filled with people. Everything on it seemed to be locked for the night.

The air stung her nose with the ripe stench of fish, but Emilia led Jacob into the shadows. The ground here was slick. Emilia tried not to think of why that would be.

"Was it the Hag?" Jacob whispered when Emilia stopped walking. "Did she send someone to kill us?"

"If the Hag had sent someone to kill us, we would be dead." Emilia peered into the shadows. Every lap of the waves sounded like a threat. "It had to be the Dragons, but how could they have gotten here so quickly? Even if they found out wizards were searching for the Siren on a hotel computer, they shouldn't be here already. We didn't do any magic big enough to trace. We've been careful. No one knows where we are."

"Marshal does," Jacob said, pulling Emilia's coat from her pack and handing it to her.

She hadn't even noticed she was shivering. "That *Demadais* rat betrayed us? How?"

"Aunt Iz lives in the same house she has for a long time. Clan wizards don't seem to move too much. Maybe Marshal went to see one of his old friends, and they let the Dragons know where we are."

"If his friend wasn't already a Dragon. I wonder if they unbound him?" She shoved her hands into her pockets for warmth, but there was already something there. Emilia pulled out the crumpled train schedule she had printed less than an hour ago.

"I think the train ride is out," Jacob said.

"*Inexuro.*" The paper caught fire. She watched as the flames that didn't burn her hand devoured the page.

But as the paper scattered as ash, something else appeared in Emilia's hand. A scroll of deep violet silk lay on Emilia's palm.

"Umm, Emi?" Jacob asked.

"I didn't do that," Emilia said as she carefully unrolled the scroll.

Inside was a message that glowed brightly in the night.

A gift to the bound. An answer to the question. Retivanesco.

"Is that a spell?" Jacob asked, reading over Emilia's shoulder.

"I've never heard of it," Emilia said. "This is from the Hag right?" She ran her fingers along the deep violet silk. It was smooth and perfect. It had to be from the Hag.

"Should we try the spell?"

A groan from the wooden wharf stopped her before she could reply.

"*Recora!*" The shout echoed through the night, and Emilia

THE SIREN'S REALM | 139

shoved Jacob to the ground as a bright gold light shot over their heads.

"*Primurgo!*" Jacob cried, and the air shimmered as a shield formed around them.

The man from the hotel strode toward them.

Emilia pressed her hand through the shield and screamed, "*Calparto!*" The wood in front of them split with a loud *crack* and splashed into the water. The man leaped back, and as the hood of his coat fell, Emilia saw it—the dragon tattoo wrapping from his cheek to his neck.

"We have been looking for you, Emilia LeFay." A smile spread across the man's face. "*Calvinis!*" The wharf beneath them began to glow hot like embers.

Jacob yanked Emilia to her feet and away from the burning wood.

"Do it," Jacob shouted.

Emilia looked down at the scroll in her hand. If this was a trap...

"Do it!"

"*Retivanesco!*" There was a flash of bright purple light.

⟿

*J*acob stumbled and fell into something hard. Pain sliced his palms and knees. He opened his eyes, blinking to force the world back into focus. Everything was spinning, spinning horribly fast.

"Emilia," he mumbled, trying to get his eyes to focus on something, anything.

"I'm here." From the quavering of her voice, she felt as ill as Jacob.

A bright light shone in front of them. And something that looked like words on a sign. But the words were moving too quickly for Jacob to read.

Jacob shook his head again. The lit sign read *Hiker's Hut Motel*, and below that glowed *Vacancy*.

Emilia pushed herself to her feet and stumbled to his side. "Where are we? This doesn't look like Newport."

She was right. Even in the dark, he could tell they were far away from the stylish seaside. The trees here were taller, and the land rougher.

Emilia's teeth chattered.

"Let's get inside," Jacob said, standing and taking Emilia's arm, leading her toward the front of the motel. A sign on the door read *Member of Acadia, Maine, Chamber of Commerce.*

"She sent us all the way here?" Jacob gaped open mouthed at the sign.

"That's not possible. A spell can't do that."

"The Hag knows magic. Really old magic. Maybe it's a lost spell," Jacob said.

"You can't disappear and reappear, because as soon as you disappear, your magic ceases to exist, making reappearing impossible. Everyone knows that."

"Well, I guess no one told the Hag."

22
LEAP OF FAITH

*L*ess than an hour later, Emilia had once again coaxed a motel clerk into giving them a room for the night. The sound of a semi driving past seeped under the motel room door. Jacob had set the alarm to allow them a few hours' sleep, but he was too tense to close his eyes for more than a few seconds. Every creak or bump in the darkness sounded like an attack.

Jacob lay still, listening to Emilia breathe steadily on his shoulder. The wood-paneled walls that adorned their room in the Hiker's Hut formed shadows that danced in the dark. It wasn't what waited for them in the morning that made him nervous. He had accepted that they were doing something dangerous. It was done. Except for the actual jumping. They still had to do that part.

Feeling Emilia next to him, breathing and safe, swept away all the nightmares he had been fighting for months. But holding her couldn't change the truth—he could have lost her. They might not have made it to this night. Everything would be all right as long as he could protect her.

But what if he couldn't?

Jacob was still staring wide eyed at the plastic grained wood when the alarm finally went off at 3 a.m., and Emilia rolled sleepily over to turn it off.

"Good morning," she mumbled to Jacob as she switched on the light. She dragged her backpack across the floor to the bathroom.

Jacob quickly piled on all of his warmest clothes. Emilia had bribed the motel clerk to pick them up at 3:15 and drive them to the start of the trail up Cadillac Mountain. The man warned them it would be a cold, hard climb, but what choice did they have?

Emilia came out of the bathroom padded in sweaters. Jacob handed her a roll and coffee from the in-room coffee maker.

"Thanks." Emilia smiled feebly, holding the cup between her hands.

"Should we leave our backpacks here?" Jacob asked, trying to swallow the dark brown liquid he had meant to be coffee.

"I don't know when we'll be back." Emilia frowned at her pack.

"They aren't heavy anyway," Jacob said, zipping his up and tossing it on his back.

"You didn't *sublevis* yours?" Emilia asked, taking the top of Jacob's backpack and testing its weight.

"Huh?" Jacob asked.

"*Sublevis*," Emilia said, and instantly his pack weighed nothing.

He could still feel it against his back, but the weight on his shoulders was gone.

"Sorry, it didn't occur to me that you wouldn't know that one. I guess I forget sometimes how new the whole wizard thing is to you."

There was a light tapping on the door. Jacob opened it to find the bleary-eyed clerk.

"You're actually awake," the clerk said in a tone of mild surprise. "Better go if you want to beat sunup."

Jacob's breath blossomed white in front of him as they walked to the clerk's car. He'd been right. It was going to be a cold climb.

"Why are you interested in the mountain?" the clerk asked as he drove through the darkness.

"School project," Emilia answered without missing a beat.

"This seems like a lot of work for a school project," the clerk yawned.

"We're very dedicated students," Emilia said.

Jacob hid his smile, gazing out the window. Emilia must be used to giving those types of explanations. She had been pretending to be human her whole life.

"There are stories about that mountain," the clerk continued, not paying attention to Emilia's reply. "The park rangers don't like to tell them, but the locals know. Weird stuff happens up there."

"Weird stuff?" Jacob asked, glancing at Emilia.

"Every once in a while, you get a crazy up here," the clerk said, "people saying they've seen ghosts jumping off the mountain. But you don't know they're ghosts till after they've jumped, because the ghosts never hit the water. There's a crazy flash, and then they're gone. I've never seen it myself." The clerk stopped his car in a tiny parking lot where a single trail broke through the trees. "But who knows? You kids might get lucky."

"I think we might," Jacob said.

"Thank you for the ride." Emilia slipped a hundred-dollar bill into the clerk's hand.

The clerk looked at the bill for a moment, seeming to war with himself. "Are you sure about this?"

"Yes," Emilia said, "I think we're going to have a great hike."

The clerk smiled broadly. "Give the motel a call when you need a ride back." He saluted and drove down the road, leaving Jacob and Emilia in the dark at the base of the mountain.

"Shall we?" Jacob asked as the taillights rounded the corner.

"Sure," Emilia said, taking the first step onto the dark path.

"Are you sure we can't use magic?" Jacob asked, straining his eyes to see the roots that covered the ground. "A nice little *inluesco* spell. I don't see anyone around, and we don't want to fall off the mountain too early."

Emilia laughed. "Not worth the risk, but…" Reaching to the ground, she picked up two sticks, shorter and fatter than Jacob's wand. She handed one to Jacob before touching her finger to the tip of her own. "*Inluescilla.*" A beam of light, bright enough to illuminate the trail, shone from the end of the stick. Emilia grinned. "Looks like a flashlight." She twisted the stick in her hand. "Just don't let any humans get too close."

Jacob examined the end of his stick before placing his finger on it and said, "*Inluescilla.*" Blue white light shot into his eyes. Jacob stumbled, blinded by the brightness.

Emilia laughed softly. "Careful there." She wrapped her arms around his waist, holding him in place until his eyes had readjusted to the dark.

"Sorry," Jacob muttered, hoping the dim light wouldn't show his embarrassed flush.

Emilia smiled and shook her head, then turned back to the mountain.

Jacob shone his light up the trail. The pale blue beam made everything seem foreign and eerie. Trees shrouded the side of the mountain, making it impossible to tell where the path led. But looking up, Jacob could see some of the stars blocked out from the night sky, silhouetting the mountain in black.

"Better get moving." Emilia started up the trail.

They walked in the dark. At first, the path was flat, packed dirt, frozen hard with the nighttime frost, but soon the trail became rocky as it began to climb up the side of the mountain, weaving back and forth in switchbacks cutting through the steep incline. In some places, even the worn trail couldn't seem to conquer the mountain. Boulders lay strewn in the path, forcing them to scramble on their hands and knees, searching for footing in the dark.

The higher they climbed, the more of the mountain they could see. Flashlights glowed in the distance as other hikers climbed the worn path, making their pilgrimage to the rising sun. The trail grew steeper still. There was more climbing than walking to be done.

Even though Jacob was in fair condition, his arms burned from pulling himself from rock to rock. Emilia puffed along behind him, not arguing when Jacob reached behind to pull her up a particularly steep rock.

Emilia paused on the side of the path, staring up at the other flashlight beams ascending. The lights looked like tiny fireflies dancing their way up the mountain. Emilia grabbed a water bottle from her pack and took a long drink before handing it to Jacob. She pulled off her gloves and breathed on her fingers. Jacob took her hands in his and rubbed them gently. Her hands felt freezing and tiny, even though his were almost numb from trying to grasp the cold stones.

"Jacob," Emilia said softly, "I need to ask you not to come with me."

Jacob snorted. "Not gonna happen, Emi. You jump, I jump. Literally." Jacob tried to keep his voice steady. There wasn't a chance in Hell he was letting Emilia go to the Siren by herself. If she was going to jump into a mystical realm, he was going to be with her.

"This could be suicide. Jacob, if we're wrong…" Emilia gazed up the mountain.

"We're not. And if for some impossible reason we are, you do some quick spellwork, and we'll be fine. I'm sure you know a great spell for cushioning a death drop off the side of a mountain."

"I don't know if I can do a spell that quickly."

"Look, Emi"—Jacob took her face in his hands—"wherever you go, I go. I don't care if it's dangerous. I don't care if it doesn't end up helping us stop the Pendragon. I am going with you, and we're not going to have this conversation again." Jacob took Emilia's hands, watching as their palms began to glow gently in the greying light. "Together, Emi. That's how it's going to be."

Emilia pressed her cheek to Jacob's. "I know," she whispered, "and I'm glad. I just couldn't forgive myself if I didn't say it. I had to try." She kissed Jacob softly on the cheek before turning back to the trail and beginning the climb to the summit.

As they rounded the last bend, whispering voices drifted down to them on the biting wind. Jacob's breath caught his throat as he looked down at what they had climbed. In the dark, he hadn't realized how high they had ascended.

The faint crashing of the waves rose up through the mist that blanketed the ocean. Islands strained to peer up through the haze, as though searching for the first glimpse of the sun. Scattered around the top of the mountain, people huddled together. Emilia led Jacob through the clumps of people covered in blankets, all with their faces turned east, waiting for the sun.

The whispers of anticipation sounded like rustling leaves as they reached the cliff. Walking carefully along the ledge, Emilia stopped on an outcropping that jutted out beyond the rest of the mountaintop. The waves slammed mercilessly against the rocks far below.

Jacob tried hard not to picture Emilia or himself crashing into the rocks.

He forced himself to look away from the ledge. Pinks and golds began to paint the sky as the sun crept closer to the glowing horizon. "It's almost time," Jacob murmured, glancing at his watch. "Thirty seconds."

Emilia took his hand and laced her fingers through his.

"Twenty seconds."

Emilia looked into his eyes before taking a step closer to the edge.

The sky was orange now, shaded with brilliant reds. Any moment, the sun would come over the horizon, and night would become day.

"Ten, nine, eight, seven"—there was still time. He could pull Emilia away from the edge—"six, five, four"—they had come this far, and the Hag didn't lie—"three, two, now!" Jacob shouted, and together, he and Emilia stepped into the air.

For an instant, Jacob could hear the screams of the people who had seen them jump. He saw the new sun burst over the horizon with a brilliant green flash before everything went black.

THE SIREN'S REALM

*E*milia lay face down on something cold and hard. Panic swept through her. Her heart pounded like a drum in her ears, and her hands trembled against the ground. They had hit the rocks below the cliff. This wasn't the way to the Siren's Realm. She had been wrong.

If this was dying, though, it wasn't so bad. Nothing hurt.

But Jacob…

He would die, too. Because of her. Emilia moved her arm, trying to find Jacob's hand so he would know he wasn't alone. To her surprise, her arm slid easily over a smooth, flat surface. Wherever she was, she was not on jagged sea rocks. Emilia opened her eyes, but it was just as dark with her eyes open as it had been with them closed.

"Jacob," Emilia whispered into the darkness. "Jacob, where are you?"

She pushed herself to her knees. *"Inluesco,"* she murmured, but nothing happened. "Perfect."

She started crawling through the darkness, searching for Jacob. She crawled in circles, small at first, then getting gradually larger. If she missed Jacob in the dark, she might never find him. How big was this place?

Was this death? Being in the darkness. Trapped. Alone. Forever?

But if she were dead, would her knees be getting sore?

Emilia smacked the ground with her hand and shouted, "I just want some light!"

As though she had shouted a command, light instantly shone all around her. Emilia shielded her eyes from the sudden brightness that seemed to emanate from everywhere.

She would have thought the light came from the sky, but there was no sky. There weren't walls either, and the ground she was kneeling on wasn't any sort of floor she had seen before. The only thing she could think to compare it to was platinum. A floor of pure, smooth platinum. But there was nothing else there. Just Emilia, the floor, the light, and no Jacob.

"Jacob!" Emilia shouted, her voice echoing in the endless, empty glow. "Jacob!" He was here. She could feel him. That constant pull in her chest told her he was somewhere close by. "Jacob," Emilia whispered, closing her eyes and trying to feel where he was. "Please let me find him."

"Emilia."

She opened her eyes as Jacob wrapped his arms around her. She buried her face on his warm chest, listening to his heart beating. They were alive. "I looked, and I couldn't find you. How did you get here?"

"I don't know. I was someplace dark. I kept searching and calling for you, and then I was here." Jacob held Emilia tightly to him. "Are we dead? I thought the land of the Siren was meant to be some lush place of pleasure. This doesn't look like it to me."

"No." Emilia eased herself away from Jacob. "I think we're in the right place. I was in the dark, too, and I asked for light. I couldn't find you until I asked, and then you were standing right here."

Jacob's eyebrows scrunched together. "So we get whatever we ask for?"

"Let's try it." Emilia shrugged and turned away from Jacob to speak into the vast, glowing expanse. "I—"

"We," Jacob interrupted. "I don't want to end up in the dark again. Let's stick to *we*, okay?"

"Right." Emilia nodded. "*We* want to speak to someone who can explain this place to us."

Before a second had passed, the empty space around them filled with life. Jacob yanked Emilia out of the way as a camel raced by them, knocking both of them into a troll. The troll towered above them. Its skin was greyish-green, with a tuft of bristly black hair sticking straight out of the top of its head.

"Watch 'er feet, eh?" The troll growled and steadied a large stein of frothing blue liquid.

"Sorry, sir," Jacob stammered.

"Ma'am," Emilia corrected quickly. "He meant *ma'am*. Raised by humans," she added in a whisper with a timid smile to the troll.

The troll growled and wandered away.

"That was a woman?" Jacob asked.

"Men are bigger and have no hair," Emilia said as she looked around.

They were in a square of some kind. Wizards and creatures of every sort shoved through the crowd. All around them were silken tents in every color, with people selling food and drink.

A woman draped in a long red dress stood in the entrance to a scarlet tent, selling jewelry set with sparkling gems. A beautiful female centaur dappled in the colors of a pinto horse called to the crowd, selling spices and perfumes. Trolls, dwarves, centaurs, and wizards milled through the vendors, stopping to peruse the beautiful wares.

"Come on." Emilia took Jacob's hand and led him to the largest tent in the center of the square. It was a vivid green, trimmed with purple and embroidered with gold. A line of creatures stood outside the tent, all waiting eagerly. The dwarves peered around the legs of the centaurs, trying to get a better view of the front of the tent.

The entrance was guarded by what Emilia could only describe as a minotaur. The beast stood eight feet tall. A white cloth wrapped around his hips was the only covering on his otherwise naked body. His muscles glistened in the bright sunlight, and the head of a bull sat on his shoulders. She had heard of minotaurs but never thought she would actually see one. Let alone need to ask one for help.

"Excuse me, sir," Emilia said as calmly as she could manage. Though she had been raised as a witch, some creatures in the magical world still frightened her. "I was hoping you might be able to help us."

The minotaur looked Emilia up and down as though deciding whether to answer her question or eat her for lunch. "We can help anyone here whatever your desires are, and if you want to go in together, that's your own business. But you'll wait in line like everyone else. I don't care how fresh you are," he growled in a deep, gravelly voice.

"Actually," Jacob said, stepping between Emilia and the creature, "we're looking for someone."

"She can provide someone to fit every taste in there." The minotaur twitched his horns toward the tent. "But you'll have to wait like the rest. Services and payment will be decided inside. I'm the guard, not the salesman."

"Right, thank you." Jacob pulled Emilia a few feet away from the opening of the tent. "Do you want to wait? We can talk to whoever's inside."

Bells jingled behind them.

The minotaur drew aside the green silk flap to reveal a beautiful woman. Her silvery-blonde hair hung down to her waist. She had lips the color of raspberries, and her eyes were the same green as the tent. Her entire body shimmered as though covered in diamond dust. And the only clothing she wore was a sheath of sheer fabric that in no way veiled her nakedness.

The people waiting to get into the tent all started talking excitedly. Some even catcalled the woman, but all she did was smile an entrancing smile.

"Next please." She took the hand of the faun who was first in line. She pulled him into the tent, leaving those outside groaning in anticipation.

"Let's get out of here." Emilia grabbed Jacob's elbow, dragging him away from the tent.

"B-but," Jacob stammered as Emilia led him down the nearest alley, "we're supposed to wait in line."

Emilia turned back to him with fierceness blazing in her eyes. "There is not a chance in Hell I'm letting you near that tent. Do you know what that woman was selling?"

"Oh." Jacob blushed bright pink and examined his shoes.

"Let's find someone else to ask what's happening in this crazy place." Emilia led him farther into the maze of vendors.

She stalked through the rows of tents, trying to find someone who looked like they might be in charge. If she had been in New York City, she would have been able to find a police officer to ask for help. But here, everyone seemed intent only on enjoying themselves.

After a few minutes' walking, they came to a fountain. It was made of the same luscious metal as the floor where Emilia had woken up. In the center of the fountain was a statue of a woman, her body draped in a thin cloth. In one hand she held a goblet that poured a rich, honey-colored liquid into the fountain. Her other hand, encrusted in jewels of every color, reached to the sky and sparkled in the bright sunlight.

Around the outside of the fountain, jets of the same golden liquid arced into the air toward the woman's feet, bathing them before collecting in a swimming-pool-sized basin. Creatures of every kind danced and swam in the fountain. All of them seemed intent on drinking the liquid at the woman's feet.

A man brushed past Emilia on his way to the fountain. His dark, sleek hair was pulled back into a long ponytail. He turned to Emilia. Something in the angles of his face seemed painfully familiar.

He wore a finely cut coat and vest over a billowing white shirt. Instead of pants, the man wore dark blue britches. On his silk stocking-clad feet he wore leather shoes with large, silver buckles. Emilia had seen clothes like this in movies, but never on an actual person.

"My apologies, madam." The man gave a formal bow.

Jacob took Emilia's arm.

"Actually, could you help us?" Emilia asked. "We've just arrived, and we're a little confused."

"Assisting you would be a great honor," he said.

"Well, we've actually come here to look for someone. Do you know who I could talk to about finding her?" Emilia asked.

"My dearest lady, if you want something in this land, you need only commence on the path to finding it, and your desires will most definitely find you."

"So, if we look for her we'll find her?" Jacob asked.

"Unless finding her would break the rule of the paradox. The blessed Siren created this land for our pleasure. Here you will find eternal revelry. The Siren asks only our devotion in return. The only wish she cannot grant is one that would displease another. And if your desires cannot be met, only wait a while, and she will find something to satisfy you." The man took Emilia's hand and kissed it. "The Siren always provides."

"I still don't think I understand." Jacob stepped forward, planting himself between Emilia and the stranger, his fists tensing.

"Of course, young sir. Please follow me." The man led them to the side of the fountain. "The decree of the Siren," he said, grandly gesturing to an inscription that ran around the base of the fountain.

In the Siren's Realm a wish need only be made.
Her desire to please shall never be swayed.
But should those around you wish you ill,
the Siren's love shall protect you still.
No two blessings shall contradict,
so be sure your requests are carefully picked.
Wish for joyful pleasure to be shared by all
of the good and the brave who have risked the fall.
But a warning to you once the wish is made,
the Siren's price must always be paid.

NOTHING FOR NOTHING

*E*milia stared down at the inscription. For words that spoke of pleasure and joy, they were oddly foreboding. Before she could read through the words again, there was a loud *splash*, and she was doused in the golden liquid. Emilia sputtered and spat out a good amount of the sweet water that had flown into her mouth.

She looked around and saw a woman standing in the fountain, grinning at them. She had chestnut hair that hung around her face in wet curls.

"I have been waiting for you, Bertrand," the woman said with a coy smile.

"I am sorry to have kept you." Their escort turned back to them. "And now, my lady, I am afraid I must go. If you ever wish to find me, I assure you it will be quite possible. Only look for Bertrand Wayland, and I shall appear." Without further conversation, Bertrand kicked off his silver-buckled shoes and dove into the fountain.

Emilia watched Bertrand and the woman playing in the golden water. No wonder he looked so familiar. He was probably Dexter's great-great-great grandfather.

"So in theory, all we have to do is look for Rosalie, and we should find her," Jacob said, taking Emilia by the shoulders and steering her away from the fountain. "Might as well start now."

"Right." Emilia wrenched her gaze away from the statue of the beautiful woman. "We would like to find Rosalie Wilde." Emilia waited for the scene around them to change, but the tents surrounding them remained the same, and the sounds of laughter and splashing from the fountain did not cease.

"He said to *commence on the path to our desires.* I say we start walking."

Emilia laced her fingers tightly through Jacob's as he began to lead her down a side path of tents.

The tents here were smaller and less colorful. The light, sweet scent that Emilia had barely noticed before was replaced by something slightly stale, almost like a room whose windows had been shut for too long.

"Do you really think she's going to be in a place like this?" Emilia asked. The farther they went down the alley, the darker things seemed to become.

"I don't know." Jacob peered into the open flap of an empty tent. A table of dishes left behind from a half-eaten meal stood next to an unmade bed. "We asked to find her, and this is where we're going."

Emilia's heart sank. She didn't want to find Rosalie in a desolate place. But Rosalie had chosen to come to the Siren. Maybe this was what she wanted.

With no indication as to why, the road in front of them widened, the tents grew taller, and the fabrics richer.

"Now we're getting somewhere," Jacob said, turning to smile at Emilia.

"Or we could have gotten nowhere," Emilia said, pointing over Jacob's shoulder to the fountain of the Siren.

Jacob turned to look, and his face fell.

Bertrand Wayland was still splashing in the water, now with a redhead on either side laughing at his antics.

"Let's try another street," Jacob said, pulling Emilia through the crowd to the other side of the square. They passed a cart laden with food. The scent of roasting meat made Emilia's stomach growl.

"You hungry?" Jacob asked as though in response to Emilia's stomach's protest.

"Yes," Emilia groaned.

Jacob led her to the cart of roasting meat. There were large legs of some type of game cooking over the fire. The closer they got, the more the smell made Emilia's mouth water.

"Evenin'," the man at the meat cart called as they approached. The man, much like Bertrand, appeared out of his time. He looked like someone lost in a shipwreck at least a hundred years ago. And yet, there he stood in front of them, an older man, but very much alive.

"How much?" Emilia asked, moving to reach for her backpack, but it was gone. "My pack." She turned to Jacob. "I don't have my pack." All of their money had been in her pack. The extra food. Everything.

"I don't think either of us had them when we got here." Jacob furrowed his brow.

"The Siren don't allow earthly riches to enter her Realm. She provides for all our wants. It would be insultin' to think you could bring somethin' in here better than what she can give ya," the meat seller said.

"Then how can we get food?" Jacob asked.

"Just have to give me a draw," the man answered.

"A draw?" Emilia asked.

"A draw of yer magic. Don't get nothin' fer nothin', even here." The man held out his hand to Emilia "What's yer name girlie?"

"Emilia," she answered tentatively.

"Well, Emilia. I'm Gabriel. Now, gimme yer hand. We'll shake like friends and I'll show ya."

Emilia began to reach for the man, but Jacob knocked her hand away.

"I'll do it," Jacob said, taking the man's hand.

"Ya got a nice gentleman," the meat seller said. Their joined hands glowed for a moment. Jacob gasped, and the man released his hand. "There ya go son, one each. You both look like you need feedin'."

"Thanks," Jacob said, handing Emilia one of the two large chunks of meat before walking quickly away.

"What happened?" Emilia asked as soon as they were out of earshot.

"I don't know." Jacob shook his head and took a bite of meat. "It was like I did a spell. I could feel my magic flowing out. It usually feels like I won't ever run out of magic. But this time, I felt him take some, and there was nothing to replace it. It felt like he was sucking the magic out of me. Is that even possible?"

"Not that I've ever heard of, but I don't think things work the same way here. How long have we been here?" She looked up at the sky. The sun was already sinking low.

"I didn't think we'd been here that long." Jacob took another bite of his food. "But that would explain why we were so hungry."

"We should keep looking," Emilia said, heading toward the far end of the square. "I want to get out of this place as quickly as possible."

Emilia stopped in front of a street that held the most lavish tents they had seen yet. The sapphire blue tent on the corner was embroidered with gold, and real sapphires covered the face of the tent, making it sparkle in the fading sunlight.

"What do you think?" Emilia asked. If she had run away to a mythical land to escape all her troubles, she would want to live in a place like this.

"Might as well. We want to find Rosalie Wilde," Jacob said firmly as they started down the street.

The road they walked down was made of the same bright metal they first landed on, but this was studded with jewels. Emeralds, sapphires, peridots, and rubies all shone, creating a rainbow for them to walk upon.

Emilia's heart skipped a beat as they passed a tent made of the purest white silk studded with diamonds. The road in front of the shining white tent was embedded so thickly with diamonds that the road glittered almost unbearably, even in the pale twilight.

Emilia walked up to the tent. The flaps twisted gently in the breeze as though beckoning her in. This was it. This was what she had come to find—the most glorious place full of beauty and peace.

"Emi." Jacob grabbed her hand, roughly pulling her back. "She's not in there."

"What?" Emilia asked, confused for a moment as to who this *she* was. Emilia shook her head, trying to get her senses to right themselves.

She looked back at the tent. It still shone brightly, but as the flaps fluttered open, she could see a shadow waiting inside. A strange shadow promising comfort. And danger. But it was not Rosalie Wilde. Emilia grasped Jacob's hand and pulled him down the darkened street away from the waiting shadow.

Before they had traveled more than a dozen steps, they were in the square again, staring up at the placid face of the Siren statue. Emilia turned and walked a few steps down a side street. She couldn't stay in the square with the statue taunting her.

She found a green tent with barrels out front. She had seen the tent before, and she didn't even remember walking down this street.

"She's not here." Emilia sighed and sat down on one of the barrels. "If she were here, we would have found her already."

"Emi," Jacob said softly, pushing her hair away from her face. "We can't give up. She's here someplace."

"She's not." Emilia's voice caught in her throat. "I dragged you here for nothing. We risked our lives for nothing. We could be trapped here for nothing."

"Emilia, I know you may not want to hear this, but what if she doesn't want to be found? She ran away from your father. If she came here to hide, and that's what she most desires, then it would go against the Siren's Decree for us to find her."

"You think she doesn't want me to find her?" Tears stung Emilia's eyes.

"Not you in particular. I think she just doesn't want to be found."

"Then what do we do?"

"Sleep," Jacob said, "then work on it some more in the morning."

The sky was dark now, and the sounds of the revelry around them had shifted. Jacob was right. They should get inside.

Emilia stood and led Jacob back to the square. Before they had walked a dozen paces, a barker stepped in front of them.

"Warm bed for the night?" he asked with a grin.

"Yes, please," Jacob said. A tent flap opened to their right, and the barker ushered them through.

As soon as they stepped into the tent, the street noise disappeared. There was a washstand in one corner and a table set with food in another. In the center of the room was a large bed with red and gold silken sheets.

"Sleep well, sir." The barker reached out and shook Jacob's hand.

Jacob winced as his hand shimmered for a moment in the man's grasp.

The man dipped his chin and closed the tent flap behind him.

"You should have let me do it," Emilia said, taking Jacob's hand in her own and examining it. The golden line on his palm glowed at her touch, but she could see no sign of damage from the man drawing out Jacob's magic.

"I'd rather they take mine," Jacob said. "One of us should have their power intact, and you know a lot more magic than I do. Let them take mine."

"Be careful." Emilia brushed his palm with her thumb before dropping his hand. She walked over to the table and tore a chunk from a steaming loaf of bread, holding it out to Jacob.

"Are you sure we should eat that?" Jacob asked, eyeing the fresh bread and cheese.

"We already ate once, and I'm starving again. Besides, the decree didn't say anything about food."

Jacob took the piece of bread. "Cheers." He smiled tiredly as they both settled in at the table.

"Jacob." Emilia traced the grain of the wood in the table with her fingertip. The pattern swirled perfectly, leading her finger back to the beginning. "Do you think we can do it? This place is so much bigger than I thought it would be. And if she doesn't want to see me…"

Jacob reached across the table, taking Emilia's hand in his. "I promise you we will figure this out." Fatigue tugged at the corners of his eyes even as he smiled.

Emilia didn't know how long they had been in the Siren's Realm. It couldn't have been more than a few hours, but the sky said it had been a day. Her body said it had been a week.

"We should get some sleep," Emilia said. She brushed Jacob's cheek with her hand. Her fingers paused on the little red burn on his cheek. He had gotten that scar rescuing her. Now he was exhausted and lost, farther away from home than either of them could ever have imagined, trying to help her.

Emilia pulled Jacob up out of his seat and wrapped her arms around him, resting her head on his shoulder. His warm scent of sun and grass and life filled her. Jacob held her close, and for the first time in such a long time, Emilia felt peace. She lifted her head and kissed his cheek right next to the burn.

His breath caught as she looked into his eyes. He was so close, so very close. If she only leaned in an inch...

"Goodnight, Jacob," was all she could manage to whisper. She kicked off her shoes and climbed into the silken sheets, pulling them up over her head and closing her eyes tightly. She was asleep in moments.

~

*J*acob lay in bed, staring at the red silk tent above them. Emilia was curled up, sleeping soundly at his side, but he couldn't quiet his mind enough to sleep. His cheek still tingled from where she'd kissed him. If Emilia wanted to be with him, then he would have everything he'd ever wanted. But if it was the tethering that made her want him, he would be taking advantage of the person he cared about most, and he could never do that.

All he wanted was to be with Emilia.

No, what he wanted right now was to know if Emilia, without any spells or magic, wanted to be with him. But that was impossible. There was no way to know what she would want without magic.

Jacob dug the heels of his hands into his eyes. *Does Emilia, my Emilia, without tethering or Dragons or Sirens, want me?* The thought was rolling in his head when Emilia turned in her sleep and instinctively found the place on Jacob's chest where her head seemed to belong. Jacob smiled for a moment. Maybe the Siren was trying to tell him something. Maybe all he needed was to ask the right question. Ask for something the right way, and you can get it. His mind began to race, sorting through all the different ways to ask for the same thing, and as he congratulated himself on his own brilliance, Jacob drifted into sleep.

25

THE RIGHT QUESTION

*T*he sun's bright glow in their tent woke them the next morning. Emilia mumbled something unintelligible and stumbled over to the table, her eyes still half closed.

"Emilia," Jacob said with a smile as they sat down to breakfast. The table had magically refilled itself overnight with fruit of the brightest colors and steaming rolls. "I think I figured it out."

"Figured what out?" Emilia yawned and reached for a huge pot of steaming coffee.

"How to find your mom."

Emilia opened her mouth, but Jacob rattled on.

"We can't ask to find her, because she doesn't want to be found. But instead of asking to find her, we ask to go where people hide and do the non-magical leg work on our own."

"Do you really think that will work?" Emilia asked, her eyes widening.

"It doesn't break any of the rules in the Siren's Decree. We aren't asking her for anything that conflicts with someone else's desires. And what have we got to lose?" Jacob tossed a berry into his mouth.

"And how did you come up with this brilliant idea?"

"Let's just say it came to me in the night." Jacob grinned.

As soon as they had eaten their fill, Jacob stood up. "No time like the present, right?"

Emilia nodded and took his hand.

"We want to go where people hide."

Jacob felt the draw on his magic. There was a swirl of red silk, and everything went dim. Jacob stumbled, and Emilia grabbed his arm.

"Well, that did something," she whispered.

They stood in a dark, damp hallway in what appeared to be an abandoned factory. Rusted pipes dripped murky water onto the broken concrete floor. The dank stench of filth filled the air, like rancid water and putrid sweat. It was as different from the luxury they had just left as Jacob could imagine.

"There's no one here," Jacob whispered. "Maybe we should go. Try something else."

"May we please have a light?" Emilia asked, and instantly a glowing, green ball appeared in her palm.

She gasped, and Jacob pulled her tightly to his side. The small light Emilia held cast shadows on figures huddled on the floor of the hall. Some slept in doorways, others leaned on walls, but none of them bothered to look at the source of the light. The wizards were filthy and wearing tattered clothes, and not all of their clothes were modern. Just like the others they had met, it seemed that some of these people had been pulled out of time. A woman only feet away from them lay on the floor in a corset.

Emilia locked her fingers through Jacob's, and they started down the hall. A girl not much older than them shielded her eyes as they walked by, but she didn't speak.

Jacob looked down at her sunken face. The girl had red curls caked with mud, and her stench burned his nostrils.

"Come on." Jacob pulled Emilia down the hall. They passed dozens of dark rooms. Some were crowded with filthy figures. Others held only one. Emilia paused at every person, holding the light in her hand out to search each face. There were plenty of women and some with dark hair.

Jacob caught sight of a woman, lying spread eagle in the center of a room, laughing. It wasn't a happy laugh, but rather a high and pathetic laugh of desperation. Her face couldn't be seen from the doorway, so Emilia crept quietly into the room. The woman had short, black hair. She was pale and looked like she could be the right age, though it was impossible to tell under the layers of dirt.

Emilia stood right next to the woman when a hand reached out and grabbed her by the ankle.

"The Siren takes. Always takes, and I have nothing to give!" the woman shrieked.

Jacob wrenched Emilia away from the woman.

"I must be able to give!" she cried.

"I—I'm sorry," Emilia stammered, stumbling backward out of the room. "It's not her. The face isn't right."

Emilia jogged down the hall. Jacob chased her, unwilling to let her get more than a few feet away from him. She stopped when the hall opened up into a dark, cavernous room that smelled thickly of mold and filth. Hallways led in every direction, and scaffolding climbed all over the room. The people in this room weren't lying on the floor. They were wandering aimlessly around each other. For a moment, Jacob wondered if zombies really did exist.

"We'll never find her," Emilia said. "There are too many people. It could take weeks to search this whole place."

"Who?" A man stumbled toward them, tripping over himself so Jacob had to catch him. "Who do you wanna find? I can help. Me, I know everybody here. There's not a person in this joint I ain't met. I'm Kevin." The man reached for Emilia.

"Emilia." She didn't take the man's hand.

Jacob tried to stand the man who reeked of stale alcohol back up on his feet, but he swayed and fell onto Emilia. "Sorry, sweetheart," the man slurred. "And you?" he pointed at Jacob.

"I'm Jacob."

"Look at us being good old pals," Kevin said as Emilia heaved him up, holding onto his shoulder to keep him steady. "Friends help friends." He winked at Emilia.

"We're looking for Rosalie Wilde," Jacob said, turning Kevin away from Emilia and trying not to inhale his fumes.

"Nah, no names. I can't remember names, James. Just tell me *who* she is."

"Well," Emilia began, "she came here about seventeen years ago. She was about nineteen when she got here. And I think she looks a lot like me."

The man turned to Jacob. "Mommy issues." He nodded. "Got it. And what would she be doing here?"

"She was hiding," Jacob answered.

"All right, I got your girl. But you don't get nothin' for nothin' round here. I'll make you kids a deal. You give me a pull of magic, I find your mommy." He looked at them expectantly. "What do ya say? We got a deal?"

Jacob looked at Emilia. She bit her lip and nodded. "Deal, but you have to take us to her before you get to draw any magic."

"Not gonna happen." He shook his head. "Magic first or no deal. Come on kids. Does this look like a face that would lie?"

Jacob studied the man's face. It was barely visible under the thick layers of dirt.

"Kid, everybody down here is hungry for magic. You ain't gonna find nobody who'll help you for free." Kevin waved a hand at the people shambling around the room. More of their faces turned toward Jacob and Emilia, as though they could sense the presence of people who still had magic left in them.

"Fine, I'll give you some of my magic, but if you don't deliver, you have to deal with her." Jacob pointed to Emilia.

Emilia smiled. "You don't want to deal with me."

"Got it, no tricks here." Kevin took Jacob's hand in his.

Jacob could feel his magic being drained out of him. It was a sickening feeling, like having his life sucked out of every vein. Jacob's legs began to tremble.

"Enough." Jacob tried to pull his hand away, but Kevin held on tighter. The room started to spin, and Jacob's knees buckled. Even as he fell, the man smiled and held on.

"He said enough!" Emilia shouted, shoving Kevin backward and breaking his hold on Jacob. "Are you ok?" She helped Jacob to his feet.

"Fine." Jacob blinked, bringing the room back into focus. He looked at Kevin, but could barely recognize him. Instead of being filthy, he was dressed in a deep purple three-piece suit with shining black shoes and a matching purple hat.

"That's better," Kevin said, grinning and bouncing his shoulders. "Haven't felt like myself in a while. With a stockpile like that, the Siren's gonna treat me real good."

"Wait," Emilia said, stepping to Kevin, "take us to the woman we're looking for."

"Don't worry, kid. I don't need the karma of breaking a promise like that following me. Right this way, my lovely lady." He sauntered across the room. The other derelict wretches watched him longingly.

"Help me, sir," a woman called to Jacob. "I can trade, too!" The woman crawled after them, but Jacob didn't look back. He didn't have any more magic to spare.

Kevin whistled as he led them down a hallway like the one they had been in before. There were people lying on the ground and scattered through all the side rooms. The hallway was impossibly long. The light was so dim, the end of the corridor couldn't be seen, but they kept walking. As the minutes stretched past, Jacob wondered if the corridor even had an end. How could there be this many desperate people stuck in the darkest place of the Siren's Realm?

Finally, the man stopped outside a room. "There ya go. My duty is done, and I'm going back out to the streets."

"Why don't you use the magic to get out of here, go back home?" Jacob asked.

"Kid, the Siren's got things you wouldn't believe. I ain't never gonna leave. Time for some fun!" The man shimmered for a moment, then vanished.

"This had better be the right room," Jacob murmured, turning to Emilia, but she had already disappeared through the dark doorway.

26

ROSALIE WILDE

*E*milia walked slowly into the room. In the corner was a rusted metal bed with a young woman lying on it, curled up in a tight ball. She had long, black hair streaked with grey. Emilia ran to the bed and leaned over, desperate to see the woman's face.

"Mother?" Emilia whispered.

The woman's glazed eyes fluttered open and turned to Emilia.

Emilia stared into the face she had dreamt about so often. It was gaunt and worn. Her skin was sallow and paper-thin. Purple rings surrounded deep blue eyes that held no life in their depths. But despite all of this, Emilia recognized Rosalie Wilde.

"Mother," Emilia breathed.

"I am no one's mother," the woman croaked, laying her head back down on her arm.

"Mother, it's me. Emilia."

"I have no child," the woman mumbled.

"Aren't you Rosalie Wilde?" Jacob leaned over the bed.

The woman laughed, her voice creaking like old leather. "I might have been once. But I have not been that girl for a very long time."

"But it is you. You are Rosalie?" Emilia asked, finding it hard to breathe in the stench of the room. Rosalie did not respond. "I'm your daughter. Emilia." She pulled the sapphire pendant out of her collar. "See? You left this with me."

The woman stared for moment, blinking at the pendant. "What do you want?"

"I wanted to see you. I wanted to meet my mother."

"You have no mother."

Emilia swallowed, fighting back tears. "Yes, I do, and I have a father. And he's doing horrible things."

"How do you know him?" Rosalie snapped, struggling to sit up. Her arms shook under her slight weight.

"He found me. He captured me," Emilia said, reaching for Rosalie's arm, trying to steady her.

Rosalie jerked away, falling into the wall behind her. "I left you where he would never find you."

"I know, but he found me anyway. And he's hurting people. Killing people. I need you to help me. Please, Mother."

"I am no one's mother." Rosalie slid back down onto the filthy mattress.

"Stop saying that!" Tears rolled down Emilia's cheeks.

"I gave birth to you. That doesn't make me anyone's mother." Rosalie laughed again. Her dry laugh turned into a hacking cough.

"But you left me with Isadora Gray to protect me. That means that you loved me."

"I don't remember love anymore." Rosalie started curling back into a ball.

"Come with me. If you leave, we can find a way to get your magic back. You can be you again." Emilia knelt on the bed, reaching for Rosalie's hand.

Rosalie smiled, nestling her head back onto her arm. "Silly girl. I will never leave the Siren. Why would you even think I would want to?" Rosalie's breath slowed as she drifted back into sleep.

"She took all of your magic," Emilia said, shaking Rosalie. "She's trapping you in the dark."

"The well runs deep, runs deep, runs deep. The well runs deep and has no end," Rosalie sang softly to herself, not opening her eyes, or seeming to notice Emilia still shaking her. "The well runs deep, runs deep, runs deep." She kept singing as Jacob took Emilia's hand, drawing her away from Rosalie.

He wrapped his arm around Emilia and led her to the door. She didn't fight to stay. As they passed through the doorway, Emilia tore her gaze from her mother. She expected to see the dark and dank hallway, but instead, they stood on a balcony overlooking the ocean.

The balcony was made of white marble streaked with deep shades of purple and blue. The sun poured down around them with a light so bright Jacob's hair and skin seemed to glow. The breeze replaced the smell of stale sick with the scent of the salty ocean. It was beautiful and perfect. A sunny place she could spend the rest of her days.

Emilia felt tears running down her cheeks, their salt mixing with the taste of the ocean on her lips.

Jacob tucked her hair behind her ears "I'm sorry. I know this isn't what you wanted, but you've seen her now."

Emilia nodded, but she couldn't look at him. She had dragged him here, risked his life, for nothing.

"Emi, I think we should start trying to find a way out of here. I don't have much magic left, and we can't afford to use any of yours. We need to get out before we get stuck. There's nothing we can do here. I'm sorry we can't help your mother, but there's nothing to be gained by staying in this awful place. Let's just go."

"You're right." Emilia tossed her hair over her shoulder and strode away. She reached the door and pushed, but it wouldn't budge.

"Emilia, let me," Jacob said, but she kicked the door open before Jacob managed to catch up to her. Rosalie still lay in the corner, singing softly to herself as she slept.

"Stand up," Emilia ordered as she crossed the room. "I said stand." She grabbed her mother by the arm and tried to yank her to her feet.

"I thought you ran away from the Siren." Rosalie laughed. "I'm glad you decided to stay. Like mother like daughter."

"I am nothing like you," Emilia spat, and with a giant heave she dragged Rosalie to her feet. The woman swayed and almost fell before tumbling into Jacob's arms.

"I like you." Rosalie smiled up at him. "You're strong."

"Back off, Rosalie," Emilia growled. "Jacob, can you carry her please?"

Jacob lifted the frail woman easily and without question.

"Let's go," Emilia said.

"Go where?" Rosalie asked like a pouty infant.

"To find a way out of here."

"I'm not leaving." Rosalie started to struggle.

"I never said you had a choice," Emilia said, walking back out the door. This time she was neither in the hallway nor by the ocean. They were back in the square by the fountain.

Rosalie gasped at the bright sunlight and buried her face in Jacob's chest.

"Are you serious?" Jacob asked. "Are we really back here?"

"It's too bright." Rosalie's whine was muffled.

"Just keep your eyes closed," Emilia snapped, searching the crowds of people passing by. No one seemed at all concerned about the filthy person huddled in Jacob's arms.

"Put me back!" Rosalie screamed. "You have no right—"

"I have every right," Emilia hissed in her ear. "Debts need to be repaid, and you're going to help me."

Rosalie went quiet in Jacob's arms. Either she was asleep or had decided not to fight. Emilia didn't care which.

"How are we supposed to get out of here?" Jacob asked.

"I want to find someone who knows the way out of here," Emilia said loudly.

"Hello again, my Lady."

Emilia turned. Walking up behind her with a long, confident stride was Bertrand Wayland.

"I see you've found your quarry." Bertrand surveyed Rosalie's filthy form. "I can only hope that now you have her, you would like to partake in some of the many wonderful pleasures the Siren has to offer. You were in such a hurry before we had no time to become truly acquainted." Bertrand took Emilia's hand and pressed it to his lips.

"Actually," Jacob said, "we're looking for a way out of here. We have to get home."

"But this cannot be," Bertrand said, ignoring Jacob and looking deep into Emilia's eyes. "You cannot want to leave paradise so soon."

"Oh, we want to," Jacob answered. "We definitely want to leave right now. Isn't that right, Emilia?"

"Yes, it is." Emilia gave Bertrand a winning smile, trying to ignore the jolt that flew through her stomach.

"Pity," Bertrand said. His eyes looked pained for a moment before his bright smile returned. "There are ways to leave. Many have tried, and few succeed. Well, I don't know if they truly succeed, but I have not seen them again. So I hope for the best for their sake."

"What do we do?" Emilia asked.

"Go to the docks." Bertrand pointed down a narrow street on the far side of the fountain. "There will be a boat there. Ask it to take you where your heart desires."

"That's it?" Jacob asked, shifting Rosalie's weight in his arms. "All we have to do is catch a boat?"

"How can people not make it out? If it's just catching a boat…" Emilia didn't finish. Of course it wasn't just a boat.

"I'm afraid I have no answers. I have never wanted to return home." Bertrand bowed. "May your journey be pleasant and may you end it unscathed. And should you ever return to the Siren's Realm, I am always at your service." Bertrand turned and disappeared into the crowd.

"Great." Emilia ran her hands over her face. "Let's go catch a boat."

27

FOREVER

The street was narrow and winding, leading between long rows of colorful tents. Gradually, the tents became grey, and then the grey became stone. They walked between houses where the windows were grated with iron. Every few houses, the street turned, and they would be on a new path of stone. The sun sank behind the buildings, and before they passed the next row of houses, twilight surrounded them.

Jacob could hear the water lapping against stone before he could see it. A wide canal took the place of the street, running between the houses with barely enough room to walk on either side. Lights glistened out of nearby windows, reflecting their strange pattern on the water.

In front of them, drifting gently with the lapping tide, was a boat tied to a set of golden stairs.

"What do we do?" Jacob asked.

"Hello?" Emilia called into the night.

Jacob searched up and down the street. No one appeared or called out. The only response was a violin that began playing in the distance.

"I don't think we should get in there," Jacob said.

"You won't make it past the boat," Rosalie murmured.

Jacob hadn't even noticed she was awake.

"What do you mean?" Emilia asked. "Rosalie, why won't we make it past the boat? Rosalie."

But Rosalie said nothing. Jacob couldn't tell if she was asleep or only feigning so she wouldn't have to answer.

Emilia cursed. "I don't think we have a choice." She studied the boat.

Jacob followed her gaze. The boat didn't look dangerous. It was long and sleek. The outside was a shiny lacquered black, but the inside was red and plush. The floor was covered in thick, soft carpet, and in the back was a red velvet couch. On the stern of the boat was a shining statue of the same woman who graced the fountain. The more Jacob looked at the boat, the more inviting it became. And the more it scared him.

"I'll go first," Jacob said. Rosalie only gave the slightest sigh as he laid her down by the edge of the water. Jacob stepped carefully into the boat. It swayed gently under his feet, but nothing happened.

Emilia helped him lift Rosalie into the boat. Jacob laid her on the floor before taking Emilia's hand as she climbed down. As soon as Emilia's feet touched the red carpet, the golden rope uncoiled itself from the ladder, and the boat began to drift down the canal.

Emilia stumbled from the sudden movement and fell into Jacob's arms.

"Sorry," she said, quickly standing up but swaying again as the boat rocked.

"Maybe we should sit," Jacob said, taking Emilia's hand and leading her to the red couch.

He sat next to her. The seat, which had seemed large enough for three people when they were standing, suddenly seemed hardly big enough to fit two. Emilia's thigh was pressed to his, and there was no space for his broad shoulders. Jacob placed his arm on the back of the seat to make room. A ledge behind the couch curved his arm, making it drape perfectly over Emilia's shoulder.

Jacob held his breath, waiting for Emilia to shrug his arm away, but instead, she sank deeper into his side, settling her head in the crook of his neck.

The boat floated them gently out of one canal and into another. There was no paddle or oar to steer, and Jacob didn't know which way might lead out of the Siren's Realm.

"Do you think this is taking us the right way?" Jacob asked.

"I think we'll have to wait and see. Shhh, listen." As Emilia spoke the violin music they had heard before floated back to them as though carried by the water itself. "Isn't it beautiful?"

With a tiny sigh, she melted into Jacob's side.

He rested his cheek on her head, looking up at the stars visible between the buildings. He didn't recognize any of the constellations. Maybe the stars were different here. Maybe the stars here were hiding, too.

A cool breeze whispered around them, blowing the scent of Emilia's hair into his lungs. Lilac and sunshine. Emilia shivered, and he wrapped his arm around her even tighter.

"This is perfect," Emilia murmured. "So peaceful."

Jacob couldn't speak. She was right. This was everything he had ever wanted. Emilia in his arms, just the two of them.

The boat continued to drift from canal to canal. The boat seemed to know where it was going. It never wavered on its path, always cutting through the water with complete calm. And wherever they floated, the music followed, the violin seeming to play of love, and rest, and eternal tranquility.

"We could stay here," Emilia said, tilting her face up to look into Jacob's eyes.

"Emilia, we have to go home."

"Why?" Emilia asked. "Why should we go back there? To fight

in a war that we didn't start? To die? Jacob, we could stay here forever. Just you and me. No LeFay, no Dragons, just us."

"Emilia—"

"What else do we need, Jacob?" Emilia's face was close to his. "If we have each other, we could be happy here. Just you and me, Jacob, forever."

Jacob searched Emilia's eyes, and he knew she meant it. Here on this boat, she was his. And he could stay like this, holding her, forever.

Emilia reached up and laced her fingers through Jacob's hair, and she kissed him, slowly and deeply.

He felt a light burning in his soul that flowed out of him and into her and back again. He put his hand on the small of her back and pulled Emilia closer, pressing her to him. His body began to hum, and for the first time in his life, Jacob felt truly complete.

His breath came more quickly as she kissed him more urgently, pulling herself onto his lap.

"Jacob," Emilia murmured.

"No," Jacob whispered. "No!" he screamed, standing up and knocking Emilia into the bottom of the boat.

The warmth in his stomach was replaced by a cold stone as he looked at Emilia lying on the red carpet with tears in her eyes.

"Emilia," Jacob said, not reaching to help her up.

"It's fine," she said, sitting up on the floor and tipping her head away from him, hiding her face behind a sheet of black hair.

"We have to find a way to leave this place. We can't stay on this boat forever. Emi, we have to go home."

"I understand," Emilia said. "There are places you want to go—"

"Emilia," Jacob whispered. "I love you." He watched Emilia freeze as he said the words. "I love you. I want to stay here with you, more than anything. But Emi, we have to go home. Claire and Connor. They're waiting for us. What will Iz think if she never hears from us again? I want to stay here, but we have to go back. For them."

Emilia stayed silent for a moment, but Jacob heard her breath shudder with tears.

"Do you mean it?" Emilia asked, turning her tear stained face to Jacob. "Do you really love me?"

"More than anything, Emilia Gray, I love you. I have always loved you." Jacob wanted to reach for her. To hold her in his arms, but he knew he wouldn't have the strength to let go. Not again.

"Without a spell?" Emilia held out her gold streaked palm. "Without a boat?"

"Without any magic."

Emilia sat for a moment, gazing out over the water. The music from the violin faded away. Jacob looked down as Rosalie began to stir on the floor. He had forgotten she was there.

"We have to get home." Emilia brushed the tears from her face. "We want to go home now!" she called into the night.

The waves lapping against the boat changed their rhythm as they emerged from the dark canal and onto the sea.

THE SIREN

*I*cy sea spray hit Emilia hard in the face, washing away the peace of the canals. The waves rocked the boat dangerously. Emilia looked behind to where the canal should have been, but there were no stone buildings in sight. Their little black boat was surrounded by an ocean that seemed to become angrier with every passing moment.

A wave hit the bow, knocking them to one side. Jacob slipped on the water that had begun to pool around their feet and fell, hitting his head hard on the side of the boat.

"Jacob!" Emilia screamed. She tried to reach for him, but another wave hit the boat. The water pulled against her, threatening to force her overboard.

Thunder crashed overhead, and a high hysterical laugh cut through the booming. Rosalie lay curled in a tight ball at the bottom of the boat, laughing as though the lightning that split the sky was an old friend she was pleased to see.

Emilia scrambled over to Jacob. He pushed himself up, still clutching the side of the boat for support.

"Jacob!" Emilia cried.

"I'm fine," Jacob shouted back, pulling Emilia down to

crouch in the bottom of the boat as another wave hit. Blood streamed down the side of Jacob's face from a gash just above his ear.

"*Pelluere!*" Emilia shouted through the wind, pressing her hand to the wound on Jacob's head, but the blood continued to flow freely down Jacob's face. She couldn't heal him.

Emilia tried to staunch the blood with her hand, but the boat rocked hard to one side, nearly tossing her overboard. Jacob grabbed her arm and pulled her to sit next to him.

"Leave it," he shouted over the gale that had grown around them when Emilia reached to the gash again. "I'll be fine."

Another wave pounded their boat, and then another. The frozen wind met with the icy chill of the water. Emilia started to shake. Jacob pulled her close, but he had no warmth left to give her.

The lightning split the sky again. In the brief moment of light, Emilia saw the inches of frozen water sloshing in the bottom of the boat. Rosalie hadn't sat up. She was still curled in the bottom of the boat, her face below the water.

"Mother!" Emilia tried to scream, but a wave crested over her, driving the breath from her body. Emilia pulled herself to her mother and lifted her head above water.

Rosalie coughed and gasped.

"It's okay," Emilia screamed above the howling wind. "You'll be okay."

"Does it matter?" Rosalie whispered.

Somehow Emilia could hear every word, and they cut her like a knife.

"Emi!" Jacob shouted. He covered her with his body, trying to shield her from another wave. She hadn't felt his hand on her arm. It was as cold as the water. "We have to get out of here! We can't stay like this."

He was right. With every wave, the water in their little boat rose. Emilia was sure if she could stand, the water would be nearly to her knees. If this had been a real boat, in a real storm, would it still be afloat?

"We could ask to go back," Jacob's voice carried to her ears.

"No," Emilia shouted. "We are going to get out of here. Do you hear me?" she shouted to the storm. "We are going to get out of here!" Emilia hoped for a moment that the sky would clear, that the Siren would hear her demand and let them go. But the only response was a *crack* of thunder as loud as an explosion that shook her bones.

The sky grew darker. Waves came at them from all sides now, pounding the boat from every angle. Jacob pulled Emilia into his arms.

Emilia didn't know how long they sat freezing in the bottom of the boat, watching the water slowly rise. She waited for day to come. Or maybe this was already day. No light shone from the sky above them. Only darkness, rain, and fear.

Hours must have passed, or maybe minutes—time didn't seem to matter much in the storm. The boat was full of water to its rim, but still it floated through the violent sea, tossed by the vicious waves.

"Emi!" Jacob shouted into her ear, pulling her closer as the wind began to tear around them in circles. "The boat can't take much more of this!"

As though on cue the boat began to groan beneath them.

"We are going home! And nothing the Siren does will change our minds. I don't care how cold, or wet, or scared we are. We'd be dead by now if that's what she wanted." Emilia looked up into the sky as the deep grey shifted to a terrifying green. "Nothing you can do will change our minds! We want out!"

The wind whipped around them in tighter and faster circles. The boat creaked dangerously as it was pulled from the water and began to spin in the whirlwind. The water that had been in the bottom of the boat spilled out over the sides. Emilia fell face first into the receding water, and Jacob grabbed her around the waist to keep her from being carried overboard.

"I've got you," he screamed over the wind, pulling Emilia back down into the boat.

The rain stopped pelting their faces as it was trapped in the walls of the cyclone that lifted them into the air. Emilia tried to look down to see how high above the waves they were, but below was only a dark void. Trembling, she turned her gaze up into the green light that seemed to be drawing their boat into the angry sky.

Emilia held tight to Jacob's hand, willing the wind not to separate them.

"I'm sorry!" Rosalie shouted to the sky, prostrating herself in the bottom of the boat. "Please forgive me, Siren!"

The wind began to roar, and the green light burst brightly around them. Emilia shut her eyes, trying to block out the blinding glow. But still, through her eyelids, she could see the brilliant green. She heard a dull *thump*, and the light faded.

Emilia took a breath. They'd won. The storm was gone. But the jolt in her stomach told her Jacob was afraid—no, terrified.

Emilia opened her eyes. She looked at Jacob, but he did not look at her. He stared, his eyes wide with horror, at something behind Emilia. Emilia turned, and Jacob's fear instantly became her own.

Their boat had landed on a smooth, shining black stone floor that reflected the only source of light—a glowing green mist that hung ten feet in the air.

A woman stood in the middle of it all, mist flowing from her scalp like hair drifting through water. A thin, shimmering cloth draped loosely across her body. Emilia knew this woman, recognized the beautifully chiseled features of her face. They had found the Siren.

THE CHOICE

*R*osalie's shriek roused Emilia from her transfixed stare. The Siren was terrifying, but somehow wonderful and utterly entrancing. The boat rocked as Rosalie struggled to her feet and climbed over the side, running toward the Siren.

"Please forgive me!" she shouted.

Emilia expected the Siren to strike Rosalie down, but Rosalie continued to run until she reached the Siren and clung to the bottom of her robes, sobbing. "I have more, I can give you more!"

It wasn't until Rosalie was at her feet that Emilia realized how large the Siren was. The Siren stood at least ten feet tall and appeared unconcerned by the woman begging at her feet.

"Come," a rich female voice said.

Emilia watched the Siren's mouth move, but the sound seemed to come from all around her, drifting through the air with the green mist.

Emilia glanced at Jacob. Blood was smeared on his face and neck. His hand tightened around hers, and together they stepped out of the boat.

Emilia thought they would be to the Siren in only a few steps, but the longer they walked, the farther away the Siren became. The misty tendrils of her hair still surrounded them, radiating her deep voice. "Come."

The Siren watched them as they tried to approach, her eyes sharp but without emotion.

"Come."

Still they walked forward.

"Come."

"If you want us to come, then why won't you let us?" Jacob asked in a loud, clear voice.

The Siren's face shifted slowly into a smile, more beautiful and more terrible than any Emilia had ever seen. They took three more steps forward and were at the Siren's feet. She was even taller than Emilia had thought. Her skin was as smooth and perfect as expertly carved marble and glistened in the green light. For a moment, Emilia feared the Siren would attack. Her own terror seemed to make the Siren grow.

"We would like to go home," Jacob said.

Emilia wanted to look at him, but she was too afraid to take her eyes from the Siren.

"Your wish shall be granted." Again the Siren's mouth formed the words, but the sound of them surrounded Emilia.

"Thank you," Jacob said.

"But what if I can give you something better?" the Siren asked.

"No." Emilia shook her head.

"Your world is breaking. Fire and death are pulling it apart at the seams."

"And we have to go back to help fix it," Emilia said, fighting to keep her voice from shaking.

"I can heal your world, draw out the poison," the Siren said.

"You can?" Jacob asked.

"I can heal all things."

A tendril of green mist caressed Jacob's face, wrapping itself around his wound. His body shimmered for a moment, and when the light dimmed, the gash on his head had healed. All the blood that had stained his face was gone. It was as if he had never been hurt at all.

"I can take away the Pendragon." Her voice turned to a soft lilt as a shadow appeared in the green mist. Even with the blank, featureless face, Emilia knew it was her father.

Rosalie looked up at the figure and began to scream, covering her head and wailing into the cold black floor, but the Siren took no notice.

"I can take away everyone who would hurt you. Who would slaughter everyone you love." Figures of darkness formed behind the Pendragon, a few at first, but quickly their numbers grew until Emilia couldn't count them anymore.

"How?" Emilia asked.

"A trade," the Siren whispered. "One given to save the lives of many."

Jacob drew Emilia closer to his side, but she didn't look away from the Siren.

"You came here to find a way to defeat the Dragons. I am giving you that way. One to live in eternal light here. That is all I ask."

"Let me stay," Rosalie sobbed, pulling herself up the Siren's robe, which did not sway under Rosalie's weight but remained solid and still as stone.

"You will go. He will stay." The Siren raised a hand and pointed to Jacob as though she were Death himself.

"No!" Emilia shouted, but her voice sounded small and distant. Jacob's grip loosened on her hand. Emilia's heart raced. *Leave someone here. Leave Jacob here.*

"Emilia," Jacob said, stepping in front of her, pulling her gaze away from the Siren, "if she can do it, if she can get rid of the Dragons—"

"No, you're not staying here," Emilia said fiercely. "We want out, both of us."

"And what of those who will die? Your family? Your friends?" The shadow of the Pendragon changed. Aunt Iz stood next to Professor Eames. "What of those who will suffer torment?" A shadow appeared, lying on the ground, shrieking in unimaginable pain. "What of the humans who will die?" A thousand shadows of unknown people surrounded them, pressing in close to Emilia. She could hear each of them gasping their dying breaths. "Would you have their blood on your hands?"

"I'll stay," Emilia said, looking at the shadow of Aunt Iz. What would Aunt Iz think if she never came home?

"The trade is for one," the Siren said again, pointing to Jacob.

"And I am the one." Emilia stepped in front of Jacob.

"Emilia, no," Jacob said quietly. "I won't leave you here. I'll stay."

"Jacob—"

"I had months with you, with a family. Emi, that's more than I ever thought I would have. And knowing you're safe, that everyone is safe…Emilia, it's worth it."

Jacob took both of her hands in his. She saw tears glistening in his eyes and knew he meant it. He would stay here alone to save everyone. "Then I'll stay with you."

"One must leave," the Siren said.

"Why?" Emilia asked, her voice rising to a shriek that barely cut through the shadows.

"One must leave," the Siren repeated.

"Rosalie can go," Emilia said. Rosalie fell to the floor and screamed, writhing at the Siren's feet.

"One of the bonded." The Siren pointed to Jacob and Emilia, and both their palms flashed a bright gold.

"Then Jacob will leave," Emilia said.

"No, I won't," Jacob said.

"He has no magic. He cannot leave alone. He must stay," the Siren said.

Emilia wanted to attack, to hit the beautiful giant, but she was right. Jacob had no magic left. He had given everything he had to help Emilia.

"Emilia," Jacob whispered. He ran his fingers through her hair. "Go." He pressed his lips to her forehead.

A horrible pain ripped through Emilia's chest. She didn't know if it was her heart breaking or his.

"I can't," Emilia whispered. "I can't leave you."

"Think of Aunt Iz." His voice sounded far away, as though it were being swallowed by the mist. "She needs you." Jacob twisted her hand so the golden streak glowed in the green light. "You'll be free."

A sob rose in Emilia's throat as her soul began to tear in two.

Jacob glowed in a soft, green light. The outline of his body blurred in the mist.

"No!" Emilia shrieked. "You can't have him!"

Jacob's body was gone now. A swirl of haze had taken his place. Emilia reached into the mist where the faintest glow of gold remained. She felt her fingers lock around Jacob's. His hand felt cold and far away, something from another world where she did not belong.

"I don't want to be free!" Emilia shouted. "I don't want you to take away the Dragons." Emilia pulled with all her might, desperate to bring Jacob back from wherever the Siren had sent him. The harder she pulled, the farther away Jacob seemed to drift. "I won't let you take him." Jacob's hand began to slip from hers. "Give Jacob back! I want Jacob!"

The mist cleared, and Jacob was standing next to her, warm and real.

"I choose him." Emilia looked back to the Siren. "I won't let you keep him."

"Emi," Jacob whispered. She tightened her grip on his hand.

"You let us out of this hellhole right now. I have the magic to pay our passage. Now let us go!"

The Siren grew before them. The ceiling of the black room

rose up with her, but the mist sunk down, engulfing them. The floor beneath them shook. Emilia stumbled and felt Jacob's arms catching her.

A horrible *crack* echoed around them as the floor began to splinter. Rosalie screamed as her shadow fell through the cracks and out of sight.

"Rosalie!" Emilia screamed. But her mother was gone, swallowed by the darkness.

The ground under Emilia's feet snapped and split into a wide chasm. Jacob's arms slipped from around her as the ground beneath her disappeared. Her screams echoed as she fell into the inky blackness.

30

LOST TIME

*P*ain sliced through Jacob's lungs. He was being crushed by fire. Freezing fire, pressing in all around him. He opened his eyes, and the cold stung him, blurring his vision. He opened his mouth to scream, but salt flooded in.

Water. He was in water. Freezing cold water. Jacob searched the frozen haze, but he couldn't see Emilia anywhere. He kicked toward the light above, hoping to reach air and a way to find Emilia.

His head broke through the surface, but the air was no warmer as he desperately struggled to pull in breath. "Emilia!" he tried to scream, but his shaking lungs couldn't seem push out enough air. "Emilia!"

He searched frantically around for any sign of Emilia.

A head of black hair rose to the surface a few yards from him.

Jacob swam over as quickly as he could. "Emilia." The body floated face down in the water. He flipped her over, but it wasn't Emilia's face he saw. It was Rosalie.

"Emilia!" Jacob screamed. His heart raced in his frozen chest as he struggled to hold Rosalie's head above water while fighting the waves.

"Jacob."

He heard a faint call and looked behind him. Farther out to sea, a pale arm shot into the air over a cresting wave as Emilia swam toward him.

"Jacob!" She was swimming faster than a person should be able to, sliding over the surface of the water at an unnatural speed. Within seconds, she reached Jacob's side.

"Are you okay?" Jacob panted through chattering teeth, trying to look Emilia over for signs of damage.

"Fine," she said, looking at Rosalie, whose eyes were still shut as she lay back in the water. "We have to get her to shore."

Emilia placed her hand on Jacob's shoulder. *"Alavarus. Sustinemas."* The water around Jacob instantly warmed, and he no longer had to fight to stay afloat. Emilia placed a hand on Rosalie and repeated the spells before wrapping an arm around her chest and hauling her to shore.

Jacob swam behind, his arms cutting easily through the water, every kick propelling him forward as much as ten kicks should have. Within a minute, he had reached the shore and helped Emilia pull Rosalie onto the rocks.

"Is she breathing?" Jacob asked, pushing the wet hair out of his face.

Emilia leaned in close to Rosalie's chest. "I don't think so."

Jacob knelt down and began pressing on Rosalie's chest.

"What are you doing?" Emilia asked.

"Trying to get the water out of her lungs." Jacob leaned down to blow air into Rosalie's mouth.

"Just stop," Emilia said, dragging Jacob away from Rosalie.

"But we can save her." Jacob reached for Rosalie again, but Emilia had already laid a hand on her chest.

"Sustunda," she murmured.

A spout of water flew from Rosalie's mouth like a fountain as she began to cough. Her eyes flashed open. For a moment, she lay still, her gaze darting wildly around.

"No!" she screamed, tearing at her soaked curls. "Why would she do this? Why would she make me leave?"

"Everything is fine now, Rosalie," Emilia said, holding her mother's hands still to keep her from yanking the hair from her own head.

"Why would she make me leave? I had more than the others. Always more!" Rosalie wailed, curling herself into a tight ball as she continued to scream.

"Shh," Jacob hushed. People ran toward them on the rocky beach, shouting and waving their hands.

A woman ran at the head of the pack, sprinting in her snow boots. It wasn't until Jacob saw the woman's thick coat that he noticed the snow laying across the rocks like lace, or that he was shivering badly. Now that he was out of the water, he was freezing.

"Is she all right?" was the first of the woman's shouts that Jacob was able to understand.

"She's fine," Jacob called back. "She's breathing." Jacob turned to Emilia and whispered, "What do we do?"

Emilia shrugged. "Get rescued."

"We saw you from the far side of the beach." The woman struggled out of her coat and draped it over Emilia. "We got here as quickly as we could. Are any of you hurt?"

"Make it stop!" Rosalie screamed. "Please, I don't want to feel it again."

"Ma'am, what hurts?" a young man asked Rosalie, pulling off his coat and draping it over her.

"She's fine," Jacob said, stepping forward and tucking the coat around Rosalie. "She went into the water, and we had to get her out. She's not quite right. She doesn't understand things all the time."

An older man forced his coat around Jacob's shoulders. "We need to get you all someplace warm," the older man said, his thick white hair blowing in the wind as he crammed his own ski cap on Jacob's head. "If you think we can move her?" He looked down at Rosalie as she started to screech.

Jacob reached down and lifted Rosalie easily in his arms. Even soaking wet, she weighed little.

"Our RV is 'round here," the woman said, pointing as she herded them to a path that wound behind the beach surrounding the base of the mountain.

Jacob looked up to Cadillac Mountain rising above them. The Siren had dropped them into the water where they had jumped. Jacob's stomach seized at the sight of the jagged rocks lining the beach and shallow water. At least she hadn't let them land on that.

Rosalie twisted and whined in Jacob's arms.

"Are you sure she's all right?" the man with the wispy hair asked.

"My sister isn't well," Emilia said. "We just need to get her calmed down and home."

"Please let me go home," Rosalie moaned. "She'll take me back. I'm more than the rest of them."

"Hush, Rosalie," Emilia murmured. "Close your eyes." Emilia placed her hand on Rosalie's forehead.

Jacob heard the faintest whisper of *"Elutio"* before Rosalie's eyes crept closed, and her head slumped back onto Jacob's shoulder.

"You just have to know how to calm her down," Emilia said, smiling at the woman, who seemed concerned at Rosalie's sudden slumber.

"Here we are." The younger man pointed to an RV in a parking lot next to the trail.

He opened the door for Jacob. The warmth washed over him, stinging Jacob's frozen hands as the blood tried to flow back into them.

"Thank you," Emilia said as the wispy haired man shut the door behind her.

Jacob laid Rosalie down on the couch that lined one wall of the RV.

"I'll get something dry for you to put on." The younger man disappeared into the small room at the back.

Everything in the RV was shiny, new, and covered in Christmas decorations. Jacob watched Emilia trail her fingers along the Christmas wreath hung on the door.

"We should call a ranger," the woman said. "We need to get you to the hospital."

"That's not necessary," Emilia said. "We really are fine."

The woman's forehead wrinkled. "Are your parents in town? I'm sure they're worried sick."

"Not here, no," Emilia said, her eyes flitting to meet Jacob's. "We were on a trip on our own."

"I laid dry clothes out on the bed." The younger man returned from the back room. "You'll have to wake her up to get her out of those wet things."

"I can help," Jacob said, lifting Rosalie and heading toward the back room. Emilia moved to follow him.

"Sweetie…" the woman began.

"Emilia," Emilia said. "And this is Jacob."

"Well, I'm Dawn, and that's Eric." The woman pointed to the older man. "And Henry."

"Thank you for helping us, Dawn," Jacob said.

"Glad to," Dawn said, smiling and holding out her cell phone, "but I do think you should call your folks."

"We will," Emilia said, taking the phone and closing the door to the bedroom.

Jacob laid Rosalie on the bed.

"Jacob." Emilia held the phone out to him, her eyes wide.

"We can call Iz in a minute." Jacob turned back to Rosalie, wondering how best to get her into dry clothes. Her feet were already bare. She wore nothing but the filthy dress they had found her in.

"Jacob"—Emilia pressed the phone into Jacob's hand—"look at the date."

The screen read *December 20th*. Five days until Christmas.

"More than a month," Emilia whispered. "We were gone more than a month."

"Is that possible?" Jacob asked. "Can the Siren do that?"

"I guess so." Emilia stepped past Jacob and yanked Rosalie's dress roughly over her head. Jacob turned away as Emilia dressed her.

Jacob picked up a pair of pants from the foot of the bed and slid into them.

"Emi," he said softly, careful not to turn around.

"Yes?" she said. Her clothes hit the floor with a soft *thump*, and he closed his eyes for good measure.

"Aunt Iz—" Jacob started.

"Is going to murder us."

31

THE HIKER'S HUT

"We have to call her. We need help. We need a car. We can't keep Rosalie here, and we can't very well take her on a bus," Jacob said.

Emilia tapped him on the shoulder and he turned around. She was wearing a bright pink sweatsuit. Jacob raised an eyebrow.

"I know. Claire would never approve of this abuse of pink," Emilia said dryly.

Jacob's heart sank. Connor and Claire, left in the woods for weeks, not knowing where he and Emilia had gone. Jacob shook his head, trying to focus on the fact that they were stuck in an RV with humans, in the middle of Maine, with Emilia's crazy mother.

"We have to call Iz. We knew we'd have to face her eventually."

Emilia combed her fingers through her wet hair, gnawing on her bottom lip.

"We found your mom. We did what we set out to do."

"You're right," Emilia murmured, taking a step into Jacob and curling her head onto his chest. "I guess I never thought we would get this far. I never thought past finding her. I never thought she would be like this." Emilia swept a hand toward Rosalie, passed out on the bed in crooked sweatpants and an oversized sweatshirt.

Jacob shivered again. He couldn't tell if it was from fear of facing Aunt Iz or the numbing cold that seemed to have taken up residence in his bones.

Emilia frowned at his shaking. *"Alavarus."*

Warmth surrounded him, flowing into his frozen veins. "Thanks," he said as Emilia did the same spell on Rosalie, who didn't stir.

Jacob looked at the cell phone in his hand. There was no other way. He dialed.

Where was Iz? How long would it take her to get to them? Jacob held the phone out to Emilia as it started to ring, but she backed away, putting her hands behind her.

He held the phone up to his ear, half hoping she wouldn't answer. He should have called Professor Eames. Then the professor could have told Aunt Iz they were back.

"Hello?" Aunt Iz's voice came through the phone.

"Aunt Iz," Jacob said quietly. He thought he heard a gasp.

"Jacob? Are you all right?" Iz's voice sounded tight, and he wasn't sure if she was about to cry from relief or send a spell through the phone to murder him.

"Yes," Jacob said. "We're fine."

There was silence on the other end of the line.

"Aunt Iz, we'd like to come home."

"Where are you?" Aunt Iz asked.

Jacob struggled for a moment. There was no way to hide where they had been, not if they were going to bring Rosalie home with them. "We're in Maine. Acadia, Maine. In an RV, with humans."

"Is there a place you can wait for a car in town?" Aunt Iz asked.

"The Hiker's Hut. It's a motel," Jacob said.

"Go there immediately. Do not leave the room. Do not speak to anyone. Do not even think about disappearing again. Am I clearly understood?" Aunt Iz asked in a clipped tone. Jacob was glad she was hundreds of miles away.

"Yes ma'am, we understand." Jacob held the phone out to Emilia, but she backed away, her eyes wide.

"I will send a car immediately." Iz hung up.

Jacob sighed. "That could have gone worse."

"We should ask Dawn to drop us off in town before *she* wakes up," Emilia said quietly, sitting next to Rosalie on the bed.

"What do we do when she does wake up?" Jacob sat beside Emilia.

"Try to keep her calm," Emilia said without much conviction, taking Jacob's hand in hers.

"You kids all right?" Dawn's voice came through the door.

Emilia took a deep breath before plastering a smile on her face and opening the door. "We're great. My mother is going to come and get us. I was wondering if you wouldn't mind dropping us off in town."

It took longer to get back to the motel than Jacob had expected. A dusting of snow covered the winding roads, making them slippery for the clumsy RV.

"Are you sure you don't want to stay here with us?" Henry asked, glancing from Rosalie hanging limply in Jacob's arms to Emilia who looked exhausted and a little panicked.

"No, but thank you all so much," Jacob said, carrying Rosalie carefully down the steps and back out into the cold.

She curled herself more tightly to his chest. She was starting to wake up.

"Enjoy the rest of your trip," Emilia said as Dawn pulled her into a tight hug.

Emilia waved as they drove away. "They were nice," she said, opening the door to the motel lobby.

"Can I help you?" came the automatic response from the clerk, followed quickly by, "What's wrong with her?"

"Fell asleep in the car," Jacob said. "Too much Dramamine." He was getting better at lying quickly. Another wizard skill he had learned.

"Right," the clerk said, looking at Jacob for the first time. "I know you. You're the two kids I dropped off at the mountain a while ago. You never came back."

"We went straight home, so we decided to come back again with my sister," Emilia said. "We'd love a room for the night."

"Sure. It'll be another deposit if you want to pay cash," the clerk said, digging through papers under his desk.

Their bags hadn't reappeared with them. Or if they had, they were probably at the bottom of the ocean by now. They had no money, no IDs, no clothes except for the sweatsuits Dawn had insisted they keep. Jacob's heart sank. The box with his things from Fairfield had been in his pack. The last reminders he had of his old life were somewhere in the ocean.

"No problem." Emilia's voice pulled Jacob back to the Hiker's Hut.

Emilia reached out and took the Clerk's hand. "*Immemoris.*"

The clerk's eyes went blank as a vacant smile spread across his face.

"Great," Emilia said. "Now, I want you to give us the keys to a room. You don't need to bother checking us in. Just don't let anyone else near the room."

The clerk reached behind himself and handed Emilia a room key.

"And call and order a pizza," Jacob added. "And if you pay for it, we'll pay you back tomorrow. Just call the room, and I'll come get it once it's here."

The clerk nodded and reached over to his phone.

"Thank you." Emilia led Jacob back out of the lobby and to their room.

As soon as they were outside, Jacob whispered, "How did you do that?"

"It's a memory spell, so tomorrow he won't remember he saw us. When you do a memory spell, the mind of the person you enchant becomes very impressionable for a while." Emilia furrowed her brow. "Am I awful? He'll be fine. Really he will."

"You're not awful, just a little scary sometimes."

Emilia slid the key into the lock and opened the door to their room.

It felt like they had been in a room like this three days ago, but a month had slipped by.

Jacob laid Rosalie on the bed. She stirred fitfully like a baby half asleep. "Should you do the spell again?" Jacob asked.

Emilia ran her hands through her hair and paced the room. "I don't think we should. I don't think it would be dangerous to keep her asleep, but I want a chance to talk to her before Aunt Iz gets here."

"I can leave you two alone," Jacob said.

Emilia had spent her whole life wondering about her mother. She deserved privacy for their first talk.

"Don't go." Emilia sat next to Jacob. "Please don't go." She held Jacob's hand.

"I won't." The dim room glowed brighter as Emilia's palm began to shine.

As the light touched Rosalie's face, her eyes flickered open.

"No," she mumbled, shaking her head. She pushed herself halfway up before her arms crumpled and she sprawled back onto the mattress. "No!" Rosalie shouted, covering her eyes. "Not the light. I don't want the light." She rolled back and forth on the mattress. "Not the gold, never the gold. Never again!" Rosalie shrieked into her palms.

"Rosalie, you have to be quiet," Emilia hushed, reaching for her mother. "People might hear. They'll come looking."

"Scream and scream. It doesn't matter," Rosalie cried, slapping Emilia and shoving her away.

Emilia fell hard off the bed.

Jacob grabbed Rosalie's hands to keep her from striking Emilia again. "You will not hit Emilia," Jacob said before his throat tightened. He stared in horror at Rosalie.

"Jacob, I'm fine." Emilia pushed herself off the floor. "You can let her go. She won't hurt me."

Jacob tried to find the words to tell Emilia that none of them were fine, but his mind was stuck, transfixed by the golden streak across Rosalie's palm.

STREAKED IN GOLD

"Jacob," Emilia said again, trying to pull his hands from Rosalie's wrists. But the faint light coming from Rosalie's palm caught her eye—a golden streak that matched her own.

"He'll come. He knows I'm here now," Rosalie whispered, yanking her hand away from Jacob and cradling it to her chest.

"Who, Rosalie?" Emilia asked, fear surging in her chest. "Who knows you're here?"

"Emile," Rosalie whispered. "My sweet Emile."

Emilia looked to Jacob. She could feel his panic joining her own.

"How fast will he be able to find her?" Jacob asked, moving to the window and looking outside.

"How fast could you find me?" Emilia rubbed her thumb across the mark on her own hand. How long did they have? Would it be hours or days before the Pendragon found them? "Jacob, go wait for the pizza."

Jacob looked like he might argue for a moment before shaking his head and slipping back out into the snow. He shouldn't be here. He shouldn't have to hear this. The door clicked softly shut.

Emilia took a breath and turned to Rosalie. "I need you to help me, Rosalie," she said quietly. "I want to keep all of us safe, but you have to talk to me."

Rosalie nodded and staggered to the window to stare out at the snow-covered street.

"The mark," Emilia said, "it wasn't there before. When we were with the Siren, your hand was bare."

Rosalie didn't answer but started drawing shapes in the fog on the window that Emilia could not understand.

"Rosalie, I need to know."

Rosalie showed no signs of having heard anything.

Emilia walked over and shut the curtains. "I need you to answer me. If he knows you're here, we could be in danger. Emile could find us."

"I never asked to be rescued." Rosalie rounded on Emilia, loathing shining in her eyes. "I never asked to come back."

"There was no mark when you were with the Siren," Emilia pressed on. "Did Emile know you were there? Does he know we're here?"

"He knows I'm back. His hand will shine as brightly as mine. The light will lead him to me." For the first time, Rosalie seemed sincere, and frightened.

"When I ran away with him," Rosalie said, pacing the room like a caged animal, "we bound ourselves. He promised to love me forever. We were going to stay in the woods away from humans. Safe. Always safe. And together. Never apart. But then, he came back with blood, all covered in blood. And I could feel it. I could feel how much he hated the people he killed. It felt hot in my stomach. He knew."

Rosalie pulled at her curls. "He knew I hated it. I could smell the death on him, and he loved it. But there was something growing in me, so I ran. And I kept running. But he could feel me. He knew where I was. So I left my baby outside and ran away to the Siren so she could keep me safe. The Siren protected me. And you brought me back. You tore me away."

Rosalie hunched in the corner of the room and slid down to the floor, resting her head on the wall.

"You went to the Siren to hide from your tethering?" Emilia knelt beside Rosalie. "The spell didn't work while you were there?"

"One outside and one in," Rosalie murmured. "She'll keep you safe forever. That's why she wanted the boy. To protect him from you."

"I would never leave Jacob in a place like that." Emilia's voice shook. She could feel Jacob. He was waiting outside. He was afraid. Not for himself, but for her. What would it be like to not feel the pull in her chest? To be empty. Hollow.

Rosalie grasped Emilia's face between her hands. "Then we go together. You and me. We'll both jump. And my baby and I will live in peace together. Just the two of us. Think of it, baby. You'll never have to feel him again. We could be free forever, both of us together."

Emilia pulled away. She didn't want to look into Rosalie's face. It looked too much like her own.

"Don't you want to be with your mother?" Rosalie asked. "Isn't that why you came to find me? I can save you, little baby." She reached for Emilia.

"I came to find you so I could stop LeFay." Emilia stood and walked to the other side of the room, as far away from Rosalie as she could, trying to keep herself from yelling. "I don't need a mother."

Rosalie laughed again, curling up in a ball on the floor.

"Is he coming?" Emilia asked. "How far away is he?"

"He hasn't decided yet." Rosalie closed her eyes. "But he'll come for me. Soon."

Emilia pushed through the door and out into the freezing air, gulping it in and letting the cold burn her lungs. That was where the Pendragon had gotten the idea to tether her to Dexter. The Pendragon had been tethered himself. Where had he been when he felt the pull in his chest begin again? He would recognize the feeling now Rosalie was back even if he didn't know where she had been. Emilia tried to think back. Had there been a mark on his hand when he held her captive in those caves? She couldn't remember.

"Emi." Jacob's voice pulled her back out of the caves and into the snow. His forehead scrunched up in the center like it always did when he was worried. The pizza box in his hands steamed in the cold.

"She's tethered to the Pendragon." Hot tears rolled down Emilia's cheeks. "I thought that finding her would help. I thought she would be some strong person who would fight him, or at least help us find a way to fight him ourselves. But instead, we risked our lives trying to rescue a crazy person who didn't want to be saved at all. And now she's practically a beacon leading the Pendragon right to us. Even when Aunt Iz comes, he'll still be able to feel her." Emilia took a shuddering breath. "We can't hide her."

Jacob set the pizza box down on the railing and drew Emilia into his arms. "She may be able to help."

"Help LeFay, not us." She wrapped her arms around Jacob's waist.

"She spent sixteen years with the Siren. Give her time. Maybe her mind will clear."

"And what will she be able to tell us? What she wore to her tethering? How she was bound in the same room we were so we could be like them?" Emilia stopped short and gasped. She pulled away from Jacob, shaking her head. "I didn't mean that. I'm sorry. I didn't mean that."

"It's fine." Jacob picked the box back up. "You were both forced into something you didn't want."

"She wasn't forced into anything," Emilia said quietly.

"Right." Jacob nodded, reaching for the doorknob.

Emilia took his hand. "And I would never run away." She placed her hand on Jacob's cheek, tipping his face down to hers. Slowly, carefully, her lips brushed his.

Her heart leaped, but she fought the urge to deepen the kiss, pulling away to catch her breath instead. Her cheeks burned hot in the freezing air. Why did she have to blush now?

Jacob stared at her, his eyes wide.

"I meant what I told the Siren," Emilia whispered. "I won't leave you. Not ever. I don't want to. I want to be with you."

Jacob took a step closer. His bright blue eyes shone in the light of the lone street lamp. "Emilia," he whispered, reaching toward her.

The blast of a car horn echoed from the street as a black car sped into the parking lot.

Emilia pushed Jacob behind her, waiting to see who got out of the car, expecting to see the tall, strong shadow of Stone. But instead, a mane of greying red hair emerged from the car, surrounding the furious face of Molly.

Jacob cursed only loudly enough for Emilia to hear. Molly stalked toward them, taking long strides. The mist of her breath floated into the air, making it look as though she were about to breathe fire. In her entire life, Emilia had never seen Molly this angry.

"Molly," Jacob said, stepping forward to stand at Emilia's side as the fuming woman reached them. "Before you get angry—"

"Too late," Emilia whimpered.

"I want you to know I had a really good reason for asking Emilia to run away from the centaurs' camp with me," Jacob said.

"Don't you lie to me." Molly's voice frothed with anger. "Don't you try to cover up for her." Molly pointed a trembling finger at Emilia. "And don't either of you think Isadora will be letting you get away with any of it."

"We aren't trying to get away with anything," Emilia said. "It's a lot to explain, but Molly, we need help. We have to get home to Aunt Iz."

"So *now* you care about home!" Molly shouted. "*Now* you remember you have family who worried themselves sick about you. Who did everything they could to find you, but for all we could tell, you had fallen off the edge of the earth."

"That's not far from the truth," Jacob muttered.

"And Proteus was beside himself, too!"

The door of the motel room opened, and Rosalie stumbled out, tripping over herself and tumbling into Molly. She steadied herself, hanging on Molly's coat, before pressing her finger to Molly's lips.

"Hush, now," Rosalie cooed. "My baby girl doesn't like shouting. It will bring her daddy to come find us. And then we all fall down."

Molly stared at Rosalie, her mouth hanging open.

"I found my mother," Emilia said lamely. "She's tethered to LeFay, and he might be on his way to kill us."

"Oh for God's sake," Molly said, slapping Rosalie's hand away as she tried to play with her greying red curls. "Just get in the car, all three of you."

Emilia looked at Jacob. He shrugged and took Rosalie's elbow, leading her to the car.

Jacob moved to put Rosalie in the front seat.

"No," Molly said, taking Rosalie's arm and pushing Jacob into the front seat. "I will not have any hanky panky in the back of this car. I don't know what you've been doing for the last month, but it ends here."

"Molly"—Emilia's cheeks burned again—"it wasn't like that."

"I don't care what you think it was like. Get in the car. We're going home, and then Isadora will deal with the both of you."

Emilia struggled with Rosalie, trying to get her into the car. "Rosalie, we're taking you someplace good. Someplace where they'll know how to keep us all safe."

"Back to her?" Rosalie's eyes widened.

"I'm going back to her, and she'll help you, too," Emilia said, wondering what would happen when Rosalie found out that *her* was Aunt Iz, a witch who was furious with Emilia and Jacob, instead of the Siren.

Rosalie climbed into the car and curled up on the floor behind Jacob's seat.

"Good enough." Jacob shrugged as Molly pulled away from the motel, turning the car toward home.

33

GRAY WRATH

*M*olly didn't speak as she drove. Jacob wanted to ask her to pull over for food. He had forgotten the pizza in the snow. He waited for Molly to put gas in the car, but she didn't stop. Whether the car had a spell on it, Jacob didn't dare ask. She drove through the night in stony silence.

Jacob remembered his first drive to the Mansion House. Emilia had just told him he was a wizard. His father had just died. Samuel had driven him into the unknown. Now he knew what he was going to, and he was even more afraid.

Rosalie snored softly on the floor of the car. He wanted to talk to Emilia. They should have planned what to say to Aunt Iz. Emilia's tension pulled at his chest. She was worried about what Aunt Iz would say, too. As they passed through New Hampshire, Jacob closed his eyes and let himself drift into sleep.

The car's shuddering as they passed through the *fortaceria* woke him a few hours later. Jacob blinked at the sun shining into his eyes, unsure of how it hadn't woken him before.

"Molly?" Jacob asked as they pulled up the long driveway, his voice crackled from sleep and thirst. "Who's here?" Jacob took in his first sight of the Mansion House. It was as grand and beautiful as ever, but it seemed lonely now, empty.

"Isadora is here," Molly said tersely.

"Are Connor and Claire still—" Emilia began.

"Don't pretend to care about their whereabouts. You abandoned them in the woods," Molly snapped.

Jacob wanted to tell Molly that Connor and Claire were far safer without him and Emilia around, especially now that they had the Pendragon's *coniunx* at the house with them, but somehow it didn't seem like the right time to argue with her.

As the car stopped, Jacob expected to see Aunt Iz on the steps waiting for them, but the front door remained closed.

"Rosalie," Emilia whispered, gently shaking her mother. "Rosalie, we're here."

Rosalie began to stir as Molly got out of the car and stalked into the house, leaving them behind.

"Where are we?" Rosalie asked groggily, lifting her head to look out the car window. "This isn't right. This isn't where you were supposed to take me." She opened the car door and tumbled out onto the gravel.

"Be careful." Jacob clambered out of the car and ran around to Rosalie.

Emilia knelt next to her mother, pulling stones out of Rosalie's palms, but Rosalie didn't look at her hands or at Emilia. Her eyes darted from the steps to the house.

"I know this place," Rosalie mumbled. "I was here. I left you here."

"Yes," was Emilia's only reply, but tears caught in her voice.

"You stupid child." Rosalie shoved Emilia onto the gravel.

Jacob stepped between Rosalie and Emilia.

Rosalie lunged at him, shrieking. "I leave you here. I leave you safe, and you drag me back into this Hell!"

Rosalie looked frail, but it still took all of Jacob's strength to keep her from reaching Emilia.

"Do you want him to find you?" Rosalie shouted. "Do you want him to kill us? I lied to him. He will kill all of us! And this is your fault." Rosalie pointed her pale finger at Emilia. "It is your fault when we all die."

"*Calonox.*"

Rosalie slumped in Jacob's arms. He glanced over his shoulder to see Iz striding down the front steps.

"Aunt Iz," Emilia said, pushing herself off the ground, "I'm so sorry. I wouldn't have brought her here if I knew where else to take her."

"Who is she?" Iz asked, tipping Rosalie's head back to examine her face, not looking at Jacob or Emilia.

"She's my mother," Emilia said. "We left to try and find her. And we didn't know we had been gone this long. And we found her, but she's tethered to the Pendragon. And her mind isn't quite right, but I made her come with us. I couldn't just leave her somewhere for the Pendragon to find." Emilia paused, meeting Jacob's eyes, as though silently pleading him to say something to Iz.

"We're sorry," was all he could manage.

Iz bent down and examined Rosalie's limp hand. In the sunlight, only the faintest glimmer of gold shone.

"Jacob, put this woman in the blue room. Emilia, I would like to see you in my study." Iz turned and walked into the house without looking at either of them.

It would have been better if she had screamed. Or cried. Joyful tears at their safe return might have been nice. But at least she hadn't cursed them or kicked them out. Yet.

Emilia glanced at Jacob. Her brow furrowed as she chewed her bottom lip.

Jacob opened his mouth to speak, to call after Iz that he would go with them, but Emilia shook her head and silently followed Iz into the house.

Jacob lifted Rosalie and carried her through the front door.

The inside of the house seemed cold and hollow without Claire and Connor's constant bickering. There was no scent of fresh baked goodies coming from the kitchen. This was a different home than the one he'd left.

He found the blue room in the girl's wing and laid Rosalie down on the bed. She was breathing slowly like a child sound asleep. Aunt Iz's spell was gentler than Emilia's. Jacob wanted to go down to the kitchen and find some food, but the idea of facing Molly turned his stomach.

He closed Rosalie's door. *"Compingere."* The lock clicked softly.

Jacob considered waiting in Emilia's room so he could talk to her as soon as she was done with Iz, if Iz didn't murder them both, but he didn't want Iz or Molly to find him there. He padded down the soft carpet and up the servants' stairs to the green room. His room. He flopped down face first on the bed and was sleeping before the thought of taking off his shoes had formed in his mind.

~

*A*unt Iz sat behind her desk, staring down at her fingers, not looking at Emilia.

"Aunt Iz, I'm sorry," Emilia said quietly. "But we had to go find Rosalie. Where she was, it was horrible."

"And where was she exactly?" Aunt Iz asked, her tone level. A sure sign of danger.

"In the Siren's Realm, and time moves funny there. We thought we had only been gone for a few days, and then a month had passed."

Aunt Iz's head snapped up. "The Siren's Realm is nothing more than a fairy story. Do you sincerely expect me to believe that you went to an imaginary place to rescue your long-lost mother?"

"It's the truth. There's a way into the Siren's Realm in Acadia, Maine. That's why we were there. We found a poem, and it told us how to get in."

"You found a poem?" Iz stood and paced behind her desk. "And what made you think that your mother could be there? Or that a poem you *found* might be true?"

"Sabbe said we should find my mother. And she really was with the Siren. But we didn't know she was tethered when we were there. Her hand didn't have the mark." Emilia didn't say that hers had, or that she could have stopped the Dragons but wouldn't trade Jacob. Not even to destroy the Pendragon.

"A centaur told you to run away, to find a mythical place and a woman you had never met, and you did it?" Iz stormed back and forth, back and forth. "I thought I had raised you better than that. And to do this crazy thing, you abandon Connor, Claire, and the only safe place I could find for you. You run away with Jacob, to whom you are tethered, and you expect me to believe this was all a rescue mission?"

"But it was—"

"I should have sent Jacob away as soon as you were tethered. I should never have allowed him to stay in the house with you. You are seventeen for God's sake."

"Jacob protected me."

"Is that all he did? Two bound teenagers running away together. You will end up like your mother." Iz's cheeks flushed with anger.

"I am nothing like Rosalie," Emilia growled, standing up. "And Jacob is nothing, *nothing* like LeFay. I went to find my mother because I didn't know what else to do. It was my idea, and Jacob came along to protect me, because that's what he always does. And if you try to send him away, I will go with him."

Tears streamed gently down Emilia's face as she waited for Aunt Iz to shout. But Iz stared silently at Emilia.

"If you don't trust me, at least trust Jacob." Emilia brushed the tears off her face. "Rosalie lived in the caves at Graylock. She knows how they're set up. And she knows the Pendragon. I thought she could help us get Samuel and Larkin back. I didn't know she had lost her mind. She spent too long with the Siren, and now I don't know if we'll be able to make her tell us anything. But I really did think I was helping. I couldn't survive doing nothing anymore." Emilia turned to leave.

"I am glad you are home safe," Iz said, stopping Emilia in the doorway. "And Jacob, too. I will do what I can to protect Rosalie. Perhaps she can be useful."

"Thank you, Aunt Iz." Emilia ran to Iz and hugged her hard around the neck.

Iz held Emilia tight. "But if you or Jacob leave this house without permission, if either of you steps a single toe out of line, or even considers doing so, there will be Hell to pay."

"We won't, I promise." Emilia gave Iz's hands a quick squeeze before leaving her office and heading upstairs. She wanted to find Jacob, to tell him what Iz had said. She ran up the steps to Jacob's room as quickly as her tired and sore legs could carry her. But when she opened the door to his room, he was asleep face down, snoring loudly.

Emilia pressed her hand over her mouth, trying to stop herself from laughing. She could roll him over and sleep here until he woke up, but Iz wouldn't like that. Emilia shut the door and walked back down to her room. Jacob had been right. It did smell like lilacs. She curled up on her bed and waited for sleep to come. But her mind, though exhausted, kept racing. Her mother was in this house. Sleeping only a few feet away.

When she was little, she had always hoped her mother would come for her, not to take her away from the Mansion House or Iz, but to join their family here. Her mother would teach like the professor and help take care of all the students. Back when the Mansion House had had lots of students.

But now there were no pupils left. The family had fallen apart.

Her mother was in the house, but she had lost her mind, and there was no way to know if she would ever get it back.

Emilia lay on her back, staring at the purple canopy above her bed. As she finally slid into sleep, visions of waves and green smoke drifted through her dreams.

Emilia woke with a shriek when someone pounded on her door.

"I'm not bringing your dinner to your room." Molly's terse voice carried through the door.

Heavy footfalls thumped down the stairs.

Emilia's stomach growled its hunger. She would have to face Molly eventually, and at least this way she would get food, too.

Jacob was already seated at the kitchen table when Emilia arrived. He flashed Emilia a quick smile before regaining his solemn air as Molly rounded on them.

"Did you come to my kitchen to stand or to eat?" Molly slammed a plate down on the table at the far end, away from Jacob.

"Thank you for lunch, Molly," Emilia said somberly, sitting at the table.

"It's dinnertime," Molly said. "And if you think I'm taking food up to that woman—"

"Is Rosalie awake?" Emilia asked. She took a bite of the steaming roasted potatoes heaped on her plate. Had it really been a month since she'd eaten? How was that even possible?

"Isadora has been in to speak with her," Molly said.

"I'll take food to her," Emilia said.

"Yes, please bring dinner in bed to your mother." Molly's voice cracked. "It's very sweet of you."

Emilia stood and went to Molly, wrapping her arms around her. "I didn't go to find her because she's my mother. I went to find her because she knows the Pendragon. I thought she might be able to help us. I don't need a mother, Molly. I have you and Iz. That's all I need."

Molly pulled Emilia into a backbreaking hug and began sobbing into Emilia's hair.

"I thought the two of you had been captured or run away for good. I thought I would never see either of you again," Molly choked through her tears.

"We didn't mean to scare you," Emilia whispered. "I promise we won't do it again."

"You had better not, or next time I will peel you both like carrots and leave you out for the centaurs to roast!" Molly let go of Emilia and wiped her face on her apron. "Now, take that poor Rosalie some food. That woman's brain has been addled, and good food is the first step to fixing anything."

Jacob stood and took the plate Molly tried to hand Emilia. "I'm coming with you. You shouldn't be alone with her until we know if she's calm."

Emilia nodded. If Iz had been in to see her, Rosalie must have figured out going back to the Siren was not a possibility.

"How did it go with Iz?" Jacob asked as they walked up the stairs.

"We're still both alive." Emilia shrugged. "What are we going to do about Rosalie? We can't keep her here. The Pendragon could already be on his way. How fast do you think you would be able to find me?"

"I would already be here." Jacob paused outside Rosalie's door.

"I wouldn't have run." Emilia leaned into Jacob, letting his arms wrap around her. She sighed, for a moment completely content. She could feel Jacob's heart beating in time with her own, and their hearts began to quicken.

"Shall we," Jacob said, pulling away.

"*Compuere*," Emilia murmured, and the door opened.

34

WITHOUT MAGIC

"*W*ell, if it isn't the little heroes." Rosalie lay on the bed, curled up in a tight ball facing the door.

"How are you feeling?" Jacob shut the door behind him.

"*Compingere,*" Emilia said, and the door locked shut.

"Afraid I'll run away?" Rosalie pushed herself up to sit on the bed. "I don't know where I would go. That lovely Gray woman explained to me very clearly that if I leave this room or do anything to hurt either of you, she'll tie me out front and make me wait for Emile."

"She wouldn't do that," Emilia said.

Rosalie raised a dark eyebrow.

"I'm not saying you should try it. But I don't think she would actually give you to him," Emilia said.

Rosalie stared at Emilia. "You have Emile's eyes, you know. Your hair is straight like his, but your face is like mine."

"I'm not like either of you," Emilia said, struggling to keep her tone even.

"You're right," Rosalie said. "You're like that Gray woman. I left you with her so you would be. Part of a good family, a strong Clan. Protected and provided for. But you bound yourself to him and then ran away to find me. So I suppose there is a bit of your mother in you after all. I'm sorry I tried to leave you behind. Maybe I should have stayed. Taught you not to tether yourself, no matter how much you think you love someone."

Emilia's throat tightened, and her mind raced, trying to find words to explain.

"Emile did the spell. We were bound by accident," Jacob said. His pain radiated into Emilia's chest.

"Emile is doing horrible things. He calls himself the Pendragon. He's recruited followers, and they're killing people. He found out about me and kidnapped me. Jacob saved me. He almost died saving me."

"Leave." Rosalie glared at Jacob, waving a dismissive hand at the door.

Emilia nodded.

"Are you sure?" Jacob asked.

"I'll be fine."

"I have no talisman, and I'm not sure if I have any magic left. I'll have to look into that." Rosalie studied her hands as though expecting sparks to start flying from them. "I want to talk to my baby."

"*Compuere*," Jacob said, opening the door.

"He loves you," Rosalie said as Jacob walked out of the room. He paused for a moment before shutting the door behind him.

"Don't," Emilia murmured.

"Why? Isn't that why you brought me here? For a piece of motherly advice?" She paused, but Emilia didn't speak. "How does one accidentally get tethered? Is that like how I *accidentally* had you?"

"No." Emilia swallowed hard. "The Pendragon—"

"You mean your father." Rosalie sat forward on the edge of the bed.

"He tried to tether me to someone else. Jacob tried to stop the

THE SIREN'S REALM | 219

spell and ended up tethered to me. He saved me and got stuck with me all at the same time."

"You should have left him behind. Or better yet, killed him." Rosalie stood and paced the edge of the carpet, her eyes regaining a bit of their wild glare. "It's the only permanent way out. You wouldn't have to feel him ever again."

"I would never hurt Jacob." Emilia watched Rosalie weave around the room. "I would never, ever leave him behind."

"Why?" Rosalie asked, her eyes bright and manic.

Emilia didn't answer.

"Then he should have left you."

"He's my friend. He would never leave me either."

"Not good enough." Rosalie pounded her fists on the wall. "You don't give up your freedom because someone is your friend."

"I care about him," Emilia said. "And he cares about me."

Rosalie laughed.

"He's my best friend."

"And?" Rosalie ran to Emilia, gripping the front of her shirt. "And!"

"And I don't want to be without him," Emilia said, her eyes locked with her mother's. "We're tethered. We have to stay together. That's how it works."

"I've seen you with him. I remember seeing you when we were with *her*." Rosalie tossed her mane of black hair away from her face. "You love that boy."

"We're tethered. The spell makes me—"

"The spell makes you feel his soul. The spell makes his touch intoxicating. But you have loved him for a very long time. You want him. You want to be with him."

Emilia froze as Rosalie grabbed her hand, tracing the golden streak on Emilia's palm.

"Such a funny little mark to cause so much trouble." Rosalie gripped Emilia's hand and stared directly into her eyes. "I am tethered to Emile. I ran from him. I ran as far and as fast as I could, but he could feel me. So I left you here and tried to run more. But with the Siren, it was quiet. The only heart I could feel was mine. But you ripped me out, and now I can feel every bit of rage that flows through him. Every time I breathe, I can feel that murderer breathe. I can feel him killing people. I still love him, but even more, I hate him. And that has nothing to do with the spell."

Emilia didn't notice that Rosalie had let go of her until her mother was leaning out the window.

"I'm sorry," Emilia whispered.

"Don't apologize to me," Rosalie said, the freezing wind making her hair fly around her. "Emile knows I'm here. I can feel it. He's coming for me, and then he'll come for you. And he won't stop until he has both of us. Alive or dead, he won't care, as long as we're his. And he'll kill anyone who tries to get in his way. Especially that boy of yours. Don't tell me you're sorry. Tell all the people who are going to die to protect you."

"I won't let the Pendragon hurt any of them." Emilia shoved her hands into her pockets to keep them from trembling.

"No one has ever *let* your father do anything. I know what Emile LeFay is capable of. I watched him murder a human. He practiced spells on him before slicing him with a knife. And I did nothing. Someone who is willing to do nothing can never be a mother. A mother must have a heart. A thing I clearly lack. But what do I know? I've been far away for such a long time. Either way, we won't have to wait long to see which of us is right."

Rosalie went to the bed and crawled back into her sheets. Apparently their talk was over. Emilia closed the window. She shivered as she looked out into the darkening sky, unable to shake the feeling that something was coming.

Jacob waited for her in the hall, sitting on the floor against the wall.

"How is she?" Jacob asked, looking at the carpet instead of at Emilia.

"She says the Pendragon knows she's here."

"Well, we already knew that." Jacob ran a hand through his hair. "How could you not come for someone you were tethered to if you thought they were dead?" Jacob rubbed the spot over his heart.

"She hates him," Emilia said. "She chose to tether herself to him, and she hates him. When she figured out what a monster he was, she ran. The spell didn't take away her choice."

Emilia took Jacob's hand in hers, letting the dark hallway fill with the warm golden light. "I choose you, Jacob."

She knelt in front of Jacob and leaned in slowly. Her heart began to thrum before their lips met. She threaded her fingers through his hair, and Jacob wrapped his arms around her, pulling her close as he deepened their kiss.

This was right. Without the Siren and all her magic. This was where Emilia belonged. And it didn't matter what was coming as long as they were together.

WHAT IS COMING

*T*here's magic in the wind. That's what Ms. Gray always said. As the wind whipped around him, Dexter hoped she was wrong. The only magic that could be in the wind tonight was the darkest kind. The freezing current bit his flesh, and he knew it would only get worse.

Her arms tightened around his waist. It was time. Dexter kicked off hard and felt the broom lifting them off the ground. He didn't look back as they flew away from Mount Graylock.

Larkin shook behind him. She was too weak to use any magic of her own.

"*Alavarus,*" Dexter murmured, and the air around them warmed. It wasn't much, but hopefully it would keep his hands from freezing to the broom—assuming the broom didn't fall apart and drop them out of the sky. Dexter had found the broom in the Pendragon's collection of relics. It was a Salem original. And nothing but sheer desperation could have convinced Dexter to ride it, or to risk Larkin's life flying high over the trees.

Dexter gazed up at the stars, following the constellations home. He had always hated learning astronomy. The only part he liked was keeping his arms wrapped around Emilia.

His throat tightened. The Grays might kill him on sight. He deserved it.

He aimed for the Mansion House. He didn't know where else to go. If the Dragons caught them...

Dexter pushed the broom faster. Falling off the broom was a better fate than being caught.

Hours passed. The broom swung suddenly to one side as Larkin slumped over, hanging dangerously in the air. He grabbed her wrist and tried to tighten her hold on him. He felt her jerk awake.

"Hold on, Larkin. We're almost there." The wind carried his words away, and she showed no sign of having heard.

Dexter flew over the lights of a town. In a few miles, they would reach the house. Dexter dipped the broom, flying as low as he dared over the tops of the trees. There were no lights coming from the Gray's house. They would be blocked from view by the *fortaceria*. Larkin should be able to get through Ms. Gray's spells, but not him. Not anymore.

Dexter landed the broom outside the gates. Larkin's legs buckled beneath her. He dropped the broom and caught her around the waist.

"Thanks, kid," she mumbled, trying to push the matted blond hair from her eyes with the back of her trembling hand.

"Go up to the house." Dexter helped Larkin to the gates. "Find Ms. Gray. Tell her to let me in."

Larkin placed her hand on the wrought iron gate. It shimmered and swung open. She stumbled down the dark drive without looking back. Dexter sunk down in the snow next to the wall. All he could do now was wait.

Jacob and Emilia's journey continues in The Dragon Unbound.

JACOB AND EMILIA'S JOURNEY
CONTINUES IN THE DRAGON UNBOUND

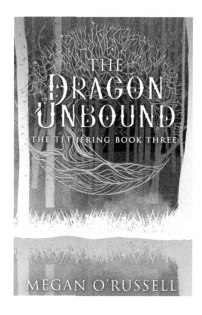

Order your copy of *The Dragon Unbound* now.

ESCAPE INTO ADVENTURE

Thank you for reading *The Siren's Realm*. If you enjoyed the book, please consider leaving a review to help other readers find Jacob and Emilia's story.

As always, thanks for reading,

Megan O'Russell

Never miss a moment of the magic and romance.

Join the Megan O'Russell mailing list to stay up to date on all the action by visiting https://www.meganorussell.com/book-signup.

ABOUT THE AUTHOR

 Megan O'Russell is the author of several Young Adult series that invite readers to escape into worlds of adventure. From *Girl of Glass*, which blends dystopian darkness with the heart-pounding danger of vampires, to *Ena of Ilbrea*, which draws readers into an epic world of magic and assassins.

With the *Girl of Glass* series, *The Tethering* series, *The Chronicles of Maggie Trent*, *The Tale of Bryant Adams*, the *Ena of Ilbrea* series, and several more projects planned for 2020, there are always exciting new books on the horizon. To be the first to hear about new releases, free short stories, and giveaways, sign up for Megan's newsletter by visiting the following:

https://www.meganorussell.com/book-signup.

Originally from Upstate New York, Megan is a professional musical theatre performer whose work has taken her across North America. Her chronic wanderlust has led her from Alaska to Thailand and many places in between. Wanting to travel has fostered Megan's love of books that allow her to visit countless new worlds from her favorite reading nook. Megan is also a lyricist and playwright. Information on her theatrical works can be found at RussellCompositions.com.

She would be thrilled to chat with you on Facebook or

Twitter @MeganORussell, elated if you'd visit her website MeganORussell.com, and over the moon if you'd like the pictures of her adventures on Instagram @ORussellMegan.

ALSO BY MEGAN O'RUSSELL

The Girl of Glass Series
Girl of Glass
Boy of Blood
Night of Never
Son of Sun

The Tale of Bryant Adams
How I Magically Messed Up My Life in Four Freakin' Days
Seven Things Not to Do When Everyone's Trying to Kill You
Three Simple Steps to Wizarding Domination
Five Spellbinding Laws of International Larceny

The Tethering Series
The Tethering
The Siren's Realm
The Dragon Unbound
The Blood Heir

The Chronicles of Maggie Trent
The Girl Without Magic
The Girl Locked With Gold
The Girl Cloaked in Shadow

Ena of Ilbrea
Wrath and Wing
Ember and Stone

Mountain and Ash

Ice and Sky

Feather and Flame

Guilds of Ilbrea

Inker and Crown

Myth and Storm

The Heart of Smoke Series

Heart of Smoke

Soul of Glass

Eye of Stone

Ash of Ages

Printed in Great Britain
by Amazon